How Nebraska Saved the Union
Common Sense for a New Revolution

Visit our website at BigWalnutCreekMedia.com.

Library of Congress Cataloging-in-Publication Data is available on file.

ISBN: 978-1-62660-168-0

Printed in the United States of America

HOW NEBRASKA SAVED THE UNION

SAVED THE UNION

COMMON SENSE FOR
A NEW REVOLUTION

ANONYMOUS

"In the following pages I offer nothing more than simple facts, plain arguments, and common sense; and have no other preliminaries to settle with the reader, than that he will divest himself of prejudice and prepossession, and suffer his reason and his feelings to determine for themselves; that he will put on, or rather that he will not put off, the true character of a man, and generously enlarge his views beyond the present day."

THOMAS PAINE
DECEMBER 23, 1776

CONTENTS

FOREWORD

Too often today, we make shallow and facile evaluations of who someone is, and glorify or discount him or her, without any regard to what he or she has to say. We constantly fail to read or consider concepts on their merit, and we routinely lack the courage to stand for right if it flies in the face of our own faction's narrative. Because of this reality, I have decided to make this offering anonymously. Who I really am is irrelevant to the discussion. I have no interest in furthering the cause of one faction over another, and I have no interest in fame or recognition. My purpose here is to tell the truth, the whole truth, and advance a simple concept in the hope of saving our nation, and maybe put into motion the next step in the evolution of our democracy.

My family participated in the founding of this nation; fought for it in every major war she has faced; led as civilization followed across the map of what became the United States; and bore witness to both good and bad government policies through the centuries. I am a veteran of the military and hold multiple degrees in both business and government. I have worked on staff in the United States Senate, served as a presidential appointee and experienced elected office in my own right. I have taught both government and constitutional law, managed my own businesses and have advised on matters of leadership, crisis management and strategic planning at home and abroad.

How Nebraska Saved the Union is a short novella about how a small group of college students and common Nebraskans, inspired by nothing more than truth and a stunning new idea, band together to lead the nation out of our current political tragedy.

x

CHAPTER
ONE

WHEN THIS STORY BEGAN, there wasn't much about it that was remarkable. A Fourth of July party in a suburban neighborhood of Omaha, Nebraska, was hardly the place one would expect a revolution to begin. Well, it didn't exactly begin there. In fact, as with most important changes in the United States, it all really began in 1776. What our Founding Fathers did that year was set into motion a mindset or process, whereby the people could figure out what was in their best interest to do next. Fighting for what is right has become more-or-less common place since then—no, not easy, sometimes horribly painful, but very American. And that more than anything, is really the point of this story—a group of Nebraskans uniting around a stunningly simple set of ideas to save the nation and move the world in a better direction.

That night was seasonally warm and humid for Nebraska. An exceptionally attractive young woman made her way out the front door, down the steps of her modest home and across the yard to what was shaping-up to be quite a festive evening. She loved her new neighborhood. Everyone was so friendly and helpful. She'd had moved in only a month earlier and already some mysterious do-gooder had mowed her lawn several times. Coming home from the university in the evening and being greeted by such wonderful neighborliness brought a huge smile to her face every time. It was the perfect affirmation that her move back-home to Omaha had been the right decision.

Her neighbors, Kris and Erik Bertelson, who she had just met, invited her to their annual party only the night before. When she was house hunting several months earlier, she had felt a warm friendliness in the neighborhood that convinced her more than any other factor to buy the house. Every time she drove up the circle, there were people in their yards working or chatting with their neighbors. All went out of their way to wave and smile. After she moved in, the phenomenon continued, and now after several weeks of this outlandish kindness, she was ready to get to know the people behind the smiles.

Before she left her house, she had watched the people on their way to the party to see if she needed to make adjustments to her wardrobe or what she should bring. Back East, parties such as this would normally see women in sun dresses and men in blazers. *God Bless the practicality of Nebraska women*, she thought to herself. *Shorts and a tank tops suit me just fine, and I would prefer my neighbors get to know the real me. I'll probably be here for a long time.*

As she walked around the shrubs that separated their drives, she heard the familiar sound of Omaha's own 311 flowing from the speakers and the crowd rapping along to *Feels So Good*. As they shouted, "Peanut Beat That Thang!" She smiled broadly and said out-loud to herself, "I think I can hang-out with these folks for a while." Laughing to herself, she ventured on.

As soon as he saw her, Erik walked down the drive to greet her. He gave her a warm hello and immediately started introducing her to everyone in rapid succession. Erik was a consummate party giver. As she was still carrying her shrimp salad for the buffet, introductions were brief. He ended their tour at the buffet and pointed her toward an impressive bar. Standing adjacent to the bar was a ping pong table, where an intense game of beer pong was underway.

"Make yourself at home!" Erik said, grinning broadly, and away he went.

As familiar as this all was, times like these were difficult for Katie, or more formally, Kathryn Mary Margret Duffy. A full-on Irish drunken brawl was certainly in her pedigree and her life's experience. Her family was anything but lace-curtain Irish. However, as she had been reminded throughout her life, Katie was something special, and with that came an enormous amount of baggage. She graduated at the top of her class at Marion High School, played every sport and participated in every activity she could fit into her schedule. Even as a ruddy-faced high school girl, she was stunning. She was tall and lanky with strawberry-blond hair that had a fiery, out-of-control quality, yet always seemed perfectly in place. And her body was… well it had made more than one priest spring a collar. Everything about her was a contradiction, and her outward perfection was only a cover for the boiling poetry contained within.

The wheels of the Omaha Archdiocese assured Katie went to Creighton University on a full scholarship. This was a good thing as her father had long since drank away anything that could be considered tuition money. But, in spite of his mostly inebriated existence, he was a kind and goodhearted Irishman with a love of life that was infectious and true. He was not a responsible man, and few expected him to be, but he did love his little Katie with his whole heart.

Katie's mother passed away from pneumonia shortly before her third birthday. From her earliest memories, Katie had been responsible for both herself and her father. She learned early and fast that life did not turn the page on its own. Everything that was written depended completely on whether or not she had the ink to go on. It was Katie who took care of the household, got herself to school and a thousand other tasks that are a challenge for two committed parents. And it was Katie who tucked her father into bed at night with a loving kiss. A heroic story would have been Katie just making it through high school, but commanding the best of outcomes, as she had consistently done, was nothing less than a miracle.

While at Creighton, she developed a reputation for academic perfection and insights well beyond her years. In fact, as an upperclassman, if she missed a question on a test, there was a flurry of excitement in the department while the professor rushed to make sure it hadn't been his or her mistake. Most of the time it was. Katie loved history, especially early American history, and after graduation from Creighton, she was accepted into the graduate American History program at Princeton.

The summer before she left for graduate school, her father passed away. She wondered to herself whether he had simply willed his heart to stop rather than continuing to be a burden on her. He was laid to rest next to Katie's mother at St. Mary's Cemetery in South Omaha. Until the funeral, only Katie knew that for eighteen years he had not missed a single day visiting her grave. Owing to the lives both he and Katie had lived until that point, it was the largest attended funeral service held at Saint Bridget's in anyone's memory.

Katie went on to finish her doctorate at Princeton and was awarded the Jocobus Fellowship, the most prestigious of Princeton's honorific fellowships. Most people thought that Katie would never leave Princeton. She was well liked in both the department and the university, but life, being the way it is, forced a reevaluation and a sudden return to Omaha and Creighton University.

Beginning a new journey, she had bought a home and was attending the first social event in her new neighborhood, where she might very well spend the rest of her life. Normally, a Chablis girl, she chose a long-neck bottle of Budweiser to start her night. Somehow it seemed the right thing to do, and as she popped the top with an opener lying nearby, she observed Erik quickly cleaning up a spill on the ping pong table. A group of young kids had knocked over a couple of glasses of beer as they tore through the room. Everything seemed wild and out-of-control and yet completely as it should be. Even compared to Princeton soirees, which seemed to always be in competition for the diversity prize, this party was even more so—there were conservatives in attendance.

There were neighbors in their seventies playing Beer Pong with kids in their twenties. There was a huge African American man who Katie thought looked familiar, maybe a former Nebraska football player, downing Scotch with an older woman in gray braids that looked like she might have been at Woodstock. There was a Hispanic woman in her forties teaching a group of other women in the kitchen how to cook Chili Rellenos, while they intermittently downed shots of tequila. Next to them was an older white guy with an NRA ballcap waxing-on about illegal immigration, in between bites of a tamale the Hispanic woman had handed him. And there was a chubby Asian man wearing a *Cornhuskers* t-shirt and cowboy boots shouting at a television playing a Nebraska football rerun.

As she looked around, a woman in the kitchen finished a shot of tequila and peeled-off to introduce herself. "Hi, I'm Candy Jones," she said.

"Katie Duffy," she responded.

"Ah, Jewish girl, huh," said Candy, laughing broadly at her own joke.

"Just an Irish lass from old South 'O', I'm afraid," she responded in a thick faux brogue.

Despite being named Candy and her slightly inebriated welcome, there was a certain reserve about her, like she wasn't likely to ever say anything she didn't intend. Katie immediately recognized a quality about her—the uncommon confidence and strength of someone who was used to being in control. Probably in her mid-fifties, she had a broad, likable face with a waistline to match. She liked to laugh, and she liked to make other people laugh, but there was a clear sophistication about her.

"What do you do?" asked Candy, directly.

"I teach history," responded Katie, lightly.

"Really," said Candy. "My husband teaches history, or at least he did. He's between jobs right now. I need to get him out of the house. Driving me crazy."

"Not a lot of jobs for history teachers," Katie said, smiling.

"Where do you teach?" asked Candy.

"Creighton," said Katie.

"University?" said Candy, recognizing there was a little more to Katie than she had originally surmised.

"Yeah, just started in January," responded Katie. "Had a chance to come home and took it."

"Family still here?" asked Candy.

"No, my parents are gone, but there's quite a few extended family members and friends still around," she said.

"I'm sorry to hear about your parents," responded Candy, graciously. "At least you still have people here."

"Yeah," said Katie, with a thin smile.

Candy nodded, "Where did you do your graduate work?"

"Princeton," said Katie.

"Ohhh," said Candy, playfully touching her arm. "I've heard of that. I'm going to have to introduce you to my husband. He did a graduate degree at Harvard and a couple at Georgetown. Was teaching at the War College until last year. He wanted to come home too. His folks aren't good."

"I'd like to meet him," said Katie.

"Johnny! Johnny! Come over here," shouted Candy into the next room.

Johnny got up from the group of guys watching the game and walked over. Katie was immediately struck by how much he looked like George Clooney. He was tall, exceptionally thin for the Midwest and looked like he was a bit of a workout freak.

"Johnny, this is Katie Duffy, nice Jewish girl I just met," said Candy.

"How do you do?" said Johnny, with a joie de vivre no less pronounced than that of his wife.

"Katie is a Professor of History at Creighton—graduate work at Princeton," said Candy, smiling at her find.

"Really?" said Johnny, intrigued.

"Came home so I could be close to the College World Series," said Katie—realizing she was flirting. She contemplated feeling guilty for a moment, but still, he was quite attractive for his age. *Stop it* she thought, and then considered again how long it had been since she was with a man. She barely heard the next question.

"You must know Max Weiss," said Johnny.

"Yeah, very well," responded Katie. "How do you know Max?"

"Oh, I spent quite a bit of time in the Middle East. We met while he was working on the *The Beekeeper,*" said Johnny.

"Really?" said Katie. "Max is into some really thoughtful stuff."

"I've seen this phenomenon before, if you'll excuse me," said Candy, with an air of feigned boredom. "Nice meeting you, Katie."

"Nice meeting you too," replied Katie. Turning back to Johnny, "What where you doing in the Middle East?"

"Army," said Johnny.

"That explains the War College," responded Katie. "More of an academic or more military?"

"No, I was a full-on soldier," said Johnny. "I just took academic vacations when I had the chance."

"Well, give me a quick run-down and your connection to Omaha," said Katie, taking a long draw from her beer.

"Let me grab one of those first," said Johnny, as he took a few quick steps to the bar to retrieve one.

As he turned toward the bar, Katie noticed herself checking him out again. *My goodness* she said to herself. *I can't take me anywhere.*

When he returned, he said, "Well, I'm originally from Blair, fifth generation Nebraska farm boy. UNL for undergrad, ROTC. Came up through the Airborne, Rangers, Special Operations Commands. Ended-up on staff with General McChrystal."

"Right," said Katie. "He was the one Obama fired over the *Rolling Stone* article."

"Yeah, basically," said Johnny. "He's a good man. Great officer."

"Love to hear about that someday," responded Katie.

Johnny shrugged with a non-committal look on his face. "So, how do you like Creighton?" he asked.

"Love it," said Katie, smiling. "Really feels like home."

"So, what's your connection to Erik and Kris?" asked Johnny.

"Just moved in next door," Katie said. "My first house. Terribly excited."

"Ah, this is a great neighborhood," Johnny responded. "Super schools, and this is the friendliest circle in town."

"I know," said Katie, confirming it with a dramatic expression. "That's one of the reasons I bought the place. Every time I drove up here, fifteen people were out front waving and smiling… I thought the Realtor had planted them at first, but then it happened again and again."

"Not exactly the East coast," said Johnny, smirking.

"No, definitely not," chuckled Katie. "And somebody keeps mowing my lawn. I don't even know who it is."

"That sounds about right," said Johnny. "There are at least two or three guys I can think of who might have done it. My guess is, you'll have to catch'em in the act."

"Probably," said Katie. "So, what's your connection here?"

"Erik and I grew-up together in Blair," said Johnny, chuckling. "He's the one who started calling me Johnny. You know, Little Johnny Jones. George Cohan."

Katie feigned looking lost.

"Give My Regards to Broadway, Yankee Doodle Dandy," said Johnny.

"Oh, yeah, I've heard of those," responded Katie, putting him on.

"Must be a generation thing," said Johnny, grimacing.

They both laughed playfully making a connection.

"Creighton was on the front page of the 'Lifestyle' section today?" Johnny asked, honestly trying to recall what he'd seen.

"Oh, Professor Fletcher," responded Katie, with a sigh.

"Yeah. I didn't read the whole article, but he certainly sounds like a colorful old bird," said Johnny.

"I don't think that quite covers it, and the article didn't really do him justice either," said Katie. "Standing there in his bathrobe and Creighton baseball cap on the front page, it all kind of belies who he really is."

"Something about a series of lectures on Trump," said Johnny.

"That was the take-away from the article, but that's not really what's going on, I don't think," responded Katie.

"Do tell," said Johnny.

"Professor Fletcher is a bit eccentric," responded Katie. "But the kids absolutely love him. They line up to take his classes. Been that way since his break-down."

"What?" said Johnny.

"Oh, it's a story alright," said Katie. "Actually, a series of stories."

"I got time," said Johnny, smiling.

"Well, the Professor went to Creighton undergrad too, popular kid, went on to Yale Law."

"Whoa," interjected Johnny. "Overachiever."

"Yeah, very," responded Katie. "After law school, somehow, he ended up working as an aide to Bill Casey on the Reagan campaign. Catholic underground thing, I suspect. After the campaign, he went with him to the CIA. About the middle of Reagan's second term, before Iran-Contra heated-up, he went back to Yale to do graduate work in philosophy."

"That sounds very company," said Johnny, smirking.

"Finished a PhD and went back to the CIA in the Office of Legal Counsel under Bush the first," said Katie, a little unsure of the details she was sharing.

"Definitely sounds like there might be some interesting footnotes to that story," said Johnny.

Nodding, Katie went on, "Back in Washington, he marries a woman from a very wealthy, old Virginia family and has a couple of kids— boys. Then, he bounces back into academia again and starts teaching philosophy at Brown. Evidently, from the start, he had enemies there who didn't like his CIA or Reagan connections, but he was very popular with the students and seemed to be doing well. Then a year or two in, a female student came forward and accused him of sexual misconduct."

"Oh, shit," said Johnny, recoiling.

"Yeah," said Katie. "He denied it. The story blew-up in the papers— said there were five women who were accusing him. Because of the line-up of heinous charges against him, he had to accept a criminal plea to a couple of low-level misdemeanors or face what everyone thought were five women willing to accuse him in open court of felony harassment… His wife left him, got full custody of their kids. His career was over."

"Well, justice done," responded Johnny. "Can't feel too sorry for him."

"Except, none of it was true," said Katie.

"What?" returned Johnny, in disbelief.

"It took another four years and two civil proceedings, but the girl's story eventually fell apart. First, there were never five women, only one. Kind of a flakey girl who had, let's say an unusual relationship with Professor Fletcher's most outspoken critic. In the second civil trial, the girl's former roommate came forward and testified the girl was nuts and the entire thing was a setup. The jury was only out for a few minutes."

"Oh, my God," said Johnny, shaking his head in genuine pain.

"Yeah," said Katie. "It pisses-me-off so bad. You know, we fight like hell to protect women, and then this kind of thing happens. Everyone who reports something thereafter has lost credibility, and it ends-up hurting the very women who need to be believed."

"Yeah," said Johnny, quietly. "What about his family?"

"His wife had already remarried by that time. He had to go to court again just to see his boys, but they didn't have much memory of him. And the new guy was 'Dad' in their eyes," said Katie, sullenly. "And it only gets worse. He was unemployable as an academic."

"But he was exonerated?" exclaimed Johnny.

"All of that shit on the internet, nobody reads past the headlines. It was just over," explained Katie. "There wasn't and isn't a single academic administrator out there who will take that kind of chance, especially with so many qualified people looking for jobs."

"What year was this?" asked Johnny.

"'07 I think, maybe '08," responded Katie.

"So, what did he do?" Johnny inquired sadly.

"Went back to the CIA," explained Katie. "Apparently asked for field duty in the Middle East."

"Death wish? Wait, wait a minute… I think I know this guy," Johnny said, with a look of profound awareness suddenly coming over his face.

"If it's the same guy, I attended a briefing once that he gave. I knew his face looked familiar. He'd gone out in the tribal areas and spent months on his own, getting to know the people—right out of Kipling. Gave the best intelligence briefing I ever heard. I remember General McChrystal, who was no fan of the agency, listened for about ten minutes, kicked everyone out but a handful of his most trusted people, offered this guy a beer, and we spent the next six or eight hours and a lot more beer just listening. He didn't sugar-coat shit. Here's what you can do. Here's what you can't and why. His intel formed a big part of the rationale for the troop levels the General went to the mat for with Obama—which caused the conflict—that was probably the genesis for the *Rolling Stone* story. It's got to be the same guy... Wow."

"Wow, yourself," responded Katie, as she furrowed her brow. "I didn't know any of that. May help to explain the next part... He ended up back at his family's farm in Arlington. His brother still farms there. His sister is a doctor here in Omaha."

"He's from Arlington, Nebraska? I had no idea. This is amazing... Okay, what got him back to Creighton?" asked Johnny, completely intrigued.

"Father Lannon, the then President of Creighton and he were good friends. Evidently, they were frat brothers back in their undergrad days. So, Father Lannon got his ducks in a row and offered him a tenured teaching position. He knew the whole story and really went to bat for him," said Katie.

"Good for him," said Johnny.

"It almost cost him though. The Professor was not in good shape. He'd been suffering for a long time—loss of his family, the war, everything. He became erratic in class, and then one day about Christmas four or five years ago, he showed up in his bathrobe, ballcap and slippers, like how he was featured in the *World Herald*. Evidently, he gave an absolutely mesmerizing lecture about the future of America, mankind, the world, the whole deal. I talked to a grad student who was there. He said it was the most amazing thing he'd ever seen. Passionate, painful—right out of *Mr. Smith Goes to Washington.* Then he falls in a lump on the floor."

"No shit?" said Johnny.

"Yeah, he disappeared for the rest of that academic year but was back on the schedule the following year. Everyone had heard the story, so there was a huge number of students asking to sign up for his class—had to add sections. Anyway, the first day he showed-up to lecture with the same bathrobe and ballcap he'd worn that day, as a joke. Everyone was so tickled he's been wearing the same thing to class ever since. From everything I've heard, his lectures and classes are absolutely amazing. He'll throw out a smattering of readings in history, literature and philosophy to do each week, and then he'll just talk. No notes."

"I wouldn't mind an audit like that," said Johnny.

"You're not the only one," responded Katie. "Standing room only most days."

"So, what's the gist of it? What's going on?" asked Johnny.

"The paper made it sound like he was going to give a series of lectures blasting President Trump's legacy, but from what I gather from some of his students, that's not what it's about at all," said Katie.

"Fake news," responded Johnny, smiling.

"Don't get me started," responded Katie. "No, from what I understand, his students are behind it all. They asked him to tie together some of the things they heard in class last semester into a couple of speeches. I'm not really sure what the breakdown is, but evidently, he's got some pretty fascinating ideas. The kids are calling it 'The Society of the Robe Lectures.'"

"That's cute," smirked Johnny.

"They've been working to promote it since the end of the Spring Semester, and tomorrow's the big day," said Katie. "Evidently, a lot of students are coming back, just for the speeches."

"Really?" said Johnny. "It might be worth some time to check it out. I'd like to say 'Hello' at any rate."

"I think I'm going too," said Katie. "I'll look for you."

"Alright," responded Johnny. "Where's it going to be?"

"He's speaking from the steps of St. John's on campus," said Katie. "Eight o'clock sharp. I'll be with some other faculty and friends on the west side of the fountain."

"Cool," said Johnny. "I'm sure I'll see you."

Candy walked up about this time, and said, "Got a date already? I can't leave you for five minutes."

"Yeah, we're going to a lecture together tomorrow evening," said Johnny, winking.

"At least, you could come up with something better than that," said Candy, with a comical sneer."

"That's all I could think of on such short notice," responded Johnny, as he put his arms lovingly around his wife.

"Well, you'll have to make it up to me when we get home," said Candy, flirting.

"See you tomorrow, Katie," said Johnny, as Candy took him by the hand and danced him toward the music.

CHAPTER

T W O

JOHNNY DROVE DOWN old Highway 75, on his way from Blair to Creighton in his old Jeep Wrangler. He may have been a staff puke and then an academic for a number of years, but his heart still beat to the Airborne Ranger within. Candy wanted to get rid of that old Jeep when they moved home, but Johnny wouldn't hear of it. Driving down the old country roads with the top down always made him feel nostalgic. He had led the Recon Platoon of the 1/504 of the 82nd Airborne Division during Desert Storm. That was before Humvees were introduced, and they still used the old WWII style Jeep as their primary recon vehicle. He had eaten, slept, fought and almost died in a topless jeep. There was too much of who he was in it to ever let it go.

It was still humid at 7 PM as he drove down North 30th Street through old Florence. Passing by Miller Park, he was saddened by how rundown the neighborhood had become. He remembered playing there as a kid with his cousins who lived adjacent to the park. It was beautiful in those days, lined by well-kept homes and yards. It had changed so much, he wondered whether or not it was ever really as lovely as he remembered.

As he pulled into the Creighton campus, he was surprised at the activity for a summer night on a holiday weekend. Every parking lot was active, and all types of people were walking in the direction of St. John's. Like many others, after failing to find parking at any of the lots nearby, he was forced to park well off campus. He was surprised and amused to see smatterings of what appeared to be students dressed in bathrobes and ballcaps. Most wore shorts and t-shirts or swimsuits underneath, but all looked hot on such a warm humid night.

As Johnny climbed the steps east of the chapel, he began to doubt whether he would find Katie as planned. There were too many people. Music was playing loudly over speakers, and the event was quickly taking on the feel of a rock concert. At the fountain in front of the church, he guessed there were two to three thousand people waiting along the promenade and on the grassy areas nearby. As he walked by a large wooden box, which had stenciled on its side in large letters, "Soap Box." he smiled. Most of the people were meandering along much as he was, taking it all in and not knowing what to expect. A big sound system was playing music on speakers strategically located to give good sound coverage for the large crowd, and an army of kids clad in robes and caps were milling around in various pockets. He had not expected the large number or the logistical planning that was becoming evident.

To both of their surprise, Johnny and Katie looked up and saw each other. "Wow, I didn't expect to find you in this crowd. This is amazing," said Johnny.

"I know, right?" said Katie. "This is nuts. I heard there were students planning on coming back for this, but this is like a beach weekend."

"This takes serious planning," said Johnny. "Is the professor behind all this?"

"No," said Katie. "I'm sure he's not. I saw him in the administration building a little bit ago, and he seemed a little taken-aback."

"Then whose driving this bus?" asked Johnny.

"I'm not sure, but I think it might be Andy St. John," said Katie. "He's the CSU President, and kind of the Big Man on Campus. I know he's a very big fan of the Professor."

"Who ever heard of coming back to campus for the holidays?" said Johnny, smirking.

"That's Andy St. John up there on the chapel steps," said Katie. "He's wearing the navy-blue cap and red and white striped robe."

"Good looking boy," said Johnny.

"Yes, he is," responded Katie.

"What's that say on his cap?" asked Johnny.

Giggling, Katie said, "Oh, Captain, My Captain."

Johnny laughed in turn.

"Are you a Walt Whitman fan?" she asked.

"No, but I did see the *Dead Poets Society*," responded Johnny, continuing to laugh. "He does look like he's the one directing traffic."

"There's Professor Fletcher," said Katie. "Walking toward the sound board next to where Andy is standing."

"Yeah, I see him. Minus the beard, he looks a lot like the guy I met at Bagram Air Base," said Johnny.

"Cool," said Katie. Both of them continued to observe Professor Fletcher as he put on a microphone headset and transmitter belt under his robe. Andy seemed to be giving him instructions, but the professor seemed a little distant and not completely engaged. He gave him a reassuring pat on the back, and the Professor walked unobtrusively toward the Soap Box. As he walked down the steps, the volume of the music rose, and *Secrets* by OneRepublic began to play.

A large, powerful-looking student in a bathrobe and cap, standing next to the soapbox, smiled, gave the Professor a strong handshake and helped pull him up onto the big box. Smiles and giggles, and a din of whispers came over the crowd. Polite applause followed. A few of the students in robes and caps whooped-it-up a bit. Overall, the crowd was in a festive mood, but they quieted respectfully as Professor Fletcher began to speak.

Speech 1: Mea Culpa

He began softly and appeared as if he were contemplating whether to turn around and leave. He took a deep, bracing breath.

"You are very kind… Thank you, my friends, for turning out on such a warm night, only a day after you no doubt celebrated the Declaration of our Independence with gusto." A few snickers filtered through the crowd. Professor Fletcher smiled and paused with a look of contemplation on his face, like he was deciding what to say.

"Two-hundred and forty-six years ago, give or take, we declared our independence from Great Britain… To be accurate, we started the Revolution in April 1775; Jefferson started drafting the *Declaration* in June of 1776; the Continental Congress voted to endorse it on July 2; they didn't sign it until August; and it wasn't delivered to the King and Parliament until that November. I mention these details only to remind us all that our democracy has always been imprecise, imperfect. Mostly, it has been a series of ideas, symbols and collective actions committed by people with good intentions. However, it is not efficient. It is not all-knowing. It is frequently wrong. And its success has been totally dependent on whether or not *We the People* were paying attention, and we haven't always."

Looking around as he spoke, it seemed the Professor was slowly beginning to gain confidence in his mission.

By now, Johnny was absolutely certain that this was the man he had met in Afghanistan over a decade earlier. Even tamped down, he possessed a cool and forthright charisma that was unmistakable. When he spoke, not only was it clear that he believed everything he was saying, he projected a firm resolve that he was more than willing to defend it.

"I am gratified and frankly a little shocked to see so many of you here tonight—members of the clergy and administration, fellow professors, my good and true students, some town folk and a surprising number of first responders," he said, chuckling. "Apparently, my past behavior is somewhat suspect, and the administration chose wisely to be prepared."

Most in the know, the crowd laughed roundly at the joke. The University President and a few members of the Board of Trustees were standing together inconspicuously under a tree on the grassy knoll. They laughed along with everyone else and gave no indication of concern, although a large number of people looked their way to gauge just that.

"When I was asked to do this, I was reluctant. As many of you know I have not been optimistic about our ability to fix the problems that face our nation. They are mounting—obvious failures to anyone who understands democracy. History is against us, and every day we neglect addressing them, they become more and more insurmountable... Maybe I have just seen too much of the world, or maybe I have lost faith that anyone will stop talking long enough to listen... But, when I look into your eyes, and I see all that passion for your future—all of those dreams—I can't help but feel an overriding sense that I must at least try..."

"I am reminded of a passage from de Tocqueville. He said almost two centuries ago, 'The greatness of America lies not in being more enlightened than any other nation, but rather in her ability to repair her faults.'"

"You see my friends, *We the People,* you standing right here in front of me, have awesome and quite unimaginable power. You just don't realize it... But it is the potential for me connecting those dots for you that has given me hope."

As the Professor spoke, his voice quivered with sincerity, and slowly, the crowd grew even more quiet and focused.

"You see, my generation," said Professor Fletcher, gaining steam. "We Baby-Boomer-Buttheads have screwed-up terribly... And we started with such promise... We were the ones who first said, 'Don't trust anyone over thirty... Serious words of wisdom, as true today as they were fifty years ago."

The crowd giggled with genuine mirth.

"Think of what we accomplished back then," he said, with mounting passion. "It moves me to tears. The '60s man! We moved the world toward Civil Rights and Women's Rights. We marched and fought. We stopped a war. No one had ever done that. We put those corrupt bastards on notice and sent Nixon packing. We upset 'the good-old-boy network' and instituted real change, man. Real change..."

"But we overshot. We got arrogant. We got comfortable, and that led us to this new twilight zone of stupid... The world kept changing, maybe faster because of what we had done, and we couldn't see it. Now, we have blown it on so many levels, and we may very well have destroyed everything. At least the generation that preceded us understood when they were wrong and were ashamed. My generation seems perfectly content to ride our arrogance right off the cliff, rather than receive an idea that could save us."

"It is deeply madding for me, today, to hear members of my generation, in all of our pompous sanctimony, dismiss you, the youth, you horrible Gen Z's, for being something less than you ought to be. We diminish you. We criticize you at every turn, as if any of this was your fault... The truth is, we are nothing but aged, self-righteous fools who see nothing, understand nothing and accept responsibility for nothing. Robin William's words from *Good Will Hunting* echo in my mind: 'It's not your fault. It's not your fault...' The perceived failures of your generation, are totally the failures of my generation, as are the problems we face as a nation today..."

The Professor paused as his words fermented. Silence grew in its intensity, and the students began to look around at each other with growing eyes.

"For all of the promise and accomplishments of my generation, we failed to learn what we should have learned. We failed to teach what we should have taught, and as a result I am not sure we will make it. I'm not sure our nation will make it. We are not paying attention. We follow without thinking. We're willing to destroy ourselves, almost gleefully, for a myriad of reasons, most commonly out of our own selfishness, and we're willing to ignore or even fight against truth, if it comes into conflict with our own perfect vision of what the world ought to be. It is an absolute fact that our democracy is failing. We are sliding toward civil war or worse, and we have no one to blame but ourselves."

The words stuck in everyone's mind and any smile had long since straightened.

"The terribly ironic thing about all of this is that it is your generation—your ideas, your passion and your dreams that are going to have to save us. You're going to have to start your own revolution, no less remarkable than the '60s or even that of 1776, to fulfill the promise of our Founding Fathers. But, in order to give you something on which to build, I need to get deep about what's really going on, what's wrong with our political process—what's wrong with us. I'm not going to play favorites. I'm not on any partisan or ideological mission. I'm not going to sugar coat it, and I'm not going to bullshit you either. I'm going to tell you the truth—the whole truth... It will sound odd to you. You hear it so infrequently, or maybe you have never heard it. But I guarantee you will know it when you do. As a matter of fact, nothing I have to say is anything you don't already know. When you do get it, you will understand, maybe for the first time, just how dark and foreboding your future really is. Think of how those boys felt the night before they went into battle at Gettysburg, as they laid on the ground listening to taps play in the distance. You may not be facing musket and ball as they did, but you are facing a challenge no less daunting to your future."

"My friends, I would not put you or me through any of this, if I did not believe there was something you could do to save us... Next Friday, I will lay all of it out for you in simple and clear terms. The objective will be remarkably familiar, common sense if you like, but the strategy on how to get there will be something you have never seen or heard before. In practical terms, it will seem quite reasonable, exceptionally fair and completely plausible. It will also put you in a place where you, personally, can make it happen—if you choose. We live in a technological age where millions of people can be moved to change in a time frame that would have seemed like magic to our Founding Fathers. We can fix this. We can fix this nation. *We the People,* led by you, you terrible kids, can fix it all."

A change had been coming over the crowd as they listened. Most of the fun had dissipated into something more akin to fear. They were listening, motivated by the obvious challenge to them, personally, and their senses were becoming heightened. Whatever had been going through their minds when this whole thing began, there was a universal understanding that they needed to listen carefully. No one wanted to miss what was coming.

"I believe there was a divinity at work when the Founding Fathers wrote our Constitution. Oh, I know its failures better than most, but like everything today, we zero-in on the things we didn't get right and completely ignore the amazing wonder of the thing. It recognized human frailty and flaw, and centuries of human struggle, and it took a chance on democracy, freedom and individual rights. Think about where those guys came from. For centuries people had been controlled by monarchs and dictators, slavery had been a worldwide fact for millennia and millions of lives had been snuffed-out in the name of God. Life itself wasn't very valuable. But the Founding Fathers did something extraordinary that began to change all of that, and until recently, their gift has resulted in a consistent march toward the betterment of the world."

"The Declaration of Independence and the Constitution were writ large to control power. They wanted the House of Representatives, the body closest to the people, to be preeminent in power, but kept in check by a Senate and a President. And, within the boundaries they set, the Supreme Court through Marbury v. Madison added another layer of control—all to make it work for *We the People*. It was masterful, and deeply embedded in their intent was for it all to work together for the greater good. They wanted an open and honest collaboration between citizen representatives to find laws that made sense, where mistakes were expected in a process to learn and grow, and not as a tool to attack one's enemies. They wanted legislators to find workable and sensible compromises, and they did not want it to be competitive. They mistrusted political parties and factions for their inherent dishonesty. They liked the idea of trial and error, learning and improving… How did it go so wrong?" he asked, sadly, with a long pause.

"Veritas… truth… the mother of all virtue—our society has lost the importance of truth. Lying has become a way of life, so accepted that we have lost trust in everything. It used to be one of the most valued parts of our existence, a corner stone to everything—reputation, integrity, honor—all rested on truth. Today, kids start lying in grade school, and they quickly find that a lie is more rewarding than telling the truth. We do not hold them accountable. There are few if any ramifications. By high school and college, kids have become so good at disguising a lie, it's impossible to tell who is lying and who is not. There is no guilt. There are no signs of internal struggle. It is an integral part of who they have become, and it is destroying everything."

"Volumes have been written on who to blame, but it really doesn't matter. It has infected everything. Now, our entire society is founded on lies and liars, and worst of all is our leadership—our elected representatives. We have no one to look up to. There once was a time when open and honest debate meant working from a foundation of the whole truth and not an intentionally stilted list of talking points... *Talking Points* are inherently dishonest because they intentionally distort the truth. When winning is the only thing that matters, nothing matters. We've lost our way. Today in the United States of America, both political parties in blazing impudence to our heritage are using a distorted reality with sinister intent—to steal power and declare their own rules. And, *We the People* have been reduced to learning the truth from the number of Pinocchios—a childish game judged by yet another group of liars."

"The media, the open and free press, championed in the First Amendment to the Constitution, was specifically designed to protect us from the lies of tyranny and those covetous of raw power. It was intended to be the bastion of honesty in a dangerous and cruel world. It was intended to be the 'Fourth Estate,' an institution of external oversight for everything government wanted to do—an exalted fortress of integrity."

"When I was in high school, my journalism teacher was a retired editor from the *Des Moines Register*—*crusty, demanding, unrelenting*—exactly what you would want an editor to be. He wanted to pass on the noble demands of his calling. He taught us the famous words that were painted on the wall of Joseph Pulitzer's newsroom—*Accuracy, Accuracy, Accuracy,* and he demanded that perfection in every facet of his teaching. He would grade our stories, particularly political news stories, on whether or not he could tell if we had a bias. This was at the height of the Vietnam War and emotions were strong even in high school newsrooms. His flat-out grading policy was an automatic 'F' if he could tell that the reporter had a bias. With him integrity was absolute. He always said, 'The point of news is to allow your readers to make up their own mind through a clear representation of the facts. If you decide you need to help them make their decisions, you're cheating the process and failing to fulfill your sacred duty as a journalist. He was not joking, not even a little bit."

"The truth today is that it's all *'fake news.'* For lack of a better word, 'news' is derived purely from considerations about money and personal opinion, and all content is driven primarily by those two factors. News organizations give their audiences what they want, and they keep pitching it for ratings and an inevitable echo effect. It is a symbiotic relationship, not an informative one. Audiences vie for the bias coverage that suits them most, and the networks give it back to them in a blur of self-gratification. If news organizations try to hold to journalistic integrity, they lose audience. It is as simple as that."

"When everyone played by the rules and journalists cared deeply about their personal and organizational integrity, things worked. Today, news outlets are no more than blatant public relations wings of their respective political affiliations and platforms for personal fame— certainly not at all what was intended. When called on it, as they often have been in recent times, they protest and shout indignation at the outrageous attack on the free press, but in reality, they are every bit as bad as they appear."

"We are living in Strawberry Fields and nothing is real. Think for a moment about why you believe what you believe. I don't care if you are a libertarian, conservative, liberal, progressive, socialist or alt-whatever. How can you possibly trust anything you know? What news source, online or otherwise, commentator or politician is unbiased enough to give you both sides of the story in context? It is all about who you believe, not who is telling the truth. To be fair, there are a few good and

honest journalists still out there, but how would you know the difference? Even if you think you are fair and balanced in your sourcing,
we all gravitate to our own world view. For half of us that's conservative news outlets, and for the other half its liberal news outlets—two
completely different and intentionally crafted views of the same facts
and neither tells the whole story. The whole truth today is rarely if ever
heard, and if you did hear it, would you even recognize it? The truth is
that your view of the world is intentionally manufactured by entities
with an agenda."

"Without truth and the rest of our American ideals, we are no better
than any other nation. Many of us still hang on to the idea that our
country is special. That is no longer true. Today, the factions that our
Founding Fathers warned us about have devolved into a win-at-all-cost
army of political zealots. Corruption and manipulation dominate the
political process, and for the perpetrators, the ends justify the means...
For God's sake, don't these people understand that Machiavelli is fundamentally incompatible with democracy. No faction has moral superi-
ority over the other. No faction can see into the future. We need each
other—liberal and conservative, and if you think we don't, you are a
fool who understands nothing of history or democracy."

"Liberals are ruled by emotion and dreams of a better world. This
nation was founded by a group—by definition liberals to a man—
dreamers who dreamed of a better way to live and govern. They wrote
and enacted a constitution that would enshrine a set of ideals that would
provide a foundation to protect the people from themselves. Without
liberals, slavery would not have ended; capitalism would have taken
complete control in the 19th Century; labor unions would not have
been allowed to organize; Social Security, Civil Rights, Women's Rights,
Medicare, Medicaid and unemployment insurance—none would have
come to fruition. Liberals have always been the fertile ground of social
and governmental progress."

Emotional cheers sprang out from the crowd and many faces danced
with an expression of pride.

The professor waited for a moment and continued, "But, without conservatives holding onto to what was practical, this nation would have ceased to exist a long time ago, and none of those things I just listed would have become a reality." The professor waited again as a few conservative students had their moment of pride.

"Some things we'd like to do are immensely challenging. Some things we'd like to do take time to develop. And some things we'd like to do threaten our very survival and cannot be done no matter how long we wait. History is impossible to overcome. We cannot rewrite, relive or redo what has passed, but we can learn, grow and improve. That is the gift given to us by our Founding Fathers."

"Someday the writers of our history will call the last hundred years or so, the *Age of Ideologies*. We've tried them all—*Communism, Socialism, Fascism, Capitalism, Progressivism, Conservatism, Liberalism, Libertarianism* and the list goes on. The truth is that all ideologies have nuggets of virtue and logic, and all are completely nuts in their extreme… After a hundred years or so of warring between them, you would think we would have been smart enough to figure that out… All ideologies, without exception, are nothing more than rhetorical platitudes designed to gain power, to convince people that they exclusively know better."

"Take socialism for example. It's an easy sell to the masses. There is a strong moral logic that flows from it, and who doesn't want free stuff? But the reality is that practiced on a large scale, socialism has always brought with it totalitarian rule; death on a monumental scale; and it has never truly worked to the benefit of the people it was supposed to help. And, the whole truth, socialism has nothing to do with equality. Wherever crafty politicians have implemented it in name, *realcapital,* as I call it, lurks and operates in the shadows and always in a form without rules or balance—much more corrupt than what it replaced… Socialism, as with all ideologies, when taken to an extreme, is nothing but a false god that sells a dream that cannot be realized, and then is kept alive by an vicious underground of power and corruption."

The professor took a long pause to allow his words to grow.

"You and I, of course, understand that each of us has a certain degree of complicity in all of this. After all we are, *We the People,* and like it or not we share in our collective failure. As much as we know and have known we've been heading in the wrong direction for years, we have done little or nothing about it. We all know it. We go our way. We get our jobs. We buy our stuff, and laugh and play, but things are not stable and we see it everywhere. The most extreme of us are preparing for the apocalypse. We all kind of think they're crazy, but we're not so sure. Our favorite movies feature superheroes, because they can face impossible challenges and still bring us back from the brink of disaster. Our favorite television show is the apocalypse, where zombies, who symbolize our narcissism, mindlessly walk down the road focused only on eating the flesh of those of us who are still alive and want a future. And, our favorite books, they're all about justifying the wrong choices we make. Why doesn't someone write a book—*True Happiness Only Comes in Service to Others?* Oh, that's right, they did, but no one reads it much anymore."

"We all know we're in real trouble and the signs are everywhere. We live in a world of façade and isolation. Rather than a prayer or kiss with a loved one at night, our first and last contact of each day is our phone. Our attitudes are no longer reflective of human reality but of carefully crafted and incessant marketing campaigns. We provide the demand for the most staggering drug use in human history and the most egregious human trafficking in 200 years. At an unprecedented rate, the soldiers who protect us come home from war and find suicide a better alternative than trying to make sense of our American reality. Fifty years ago, people who wanted to kill themselves would quietly slip off to the barn or maybe the garage and quietly end their lives. Today, they blast into our places of work, entertainment, worship or our children's schools and do everything they can to kill as many as possible before they kill themselves. It has nothing to do with laws or gun control. Nor is it about insanity or fame. It's about a society that is so sick of itself, so completely out of love with one another that God is sending us a blazing message across the heavens... And still, we refuse to see."

"As I mentioned before, there is little that I have said tonight that is beyond your understanding. In fact, it is an all too familiar exercise in futility—easy to forget. We chalk it up to a harsh, changing world over which we have little power. We are just victims of our time... *bull shit!*"

The Professor's angry exclamation did not elicit laughter as one might expect but seemed to register a sharp slap across the face to all who were listening.

"To this point, the things I have mentioned are largely personal failures—things that *We the People* could theoretically fix, if we possessed enough moral and ethical courage. But the truth is the system is so rigged and so powerful none of us are in a position to stand and be counted. If we did, we most certainly would be in the gunsight of a vicious and well-funded mob... Our political process, our system of government is broken. I'm sure you've heard that phrase many times over the past few years. Indeed, in polling, ninety percent of Americans agree. Think of that in itself for a moment. In a time when we can't get 55 percent of us to agree on anything, the overwhelming majority of us know that our own political system is broken. And, personally, I think the 10 percent that didn't agree, didn't understand the question."

"But systemic problems can be fixed by systemic solutions. Ask any operations engineer... For me, the greatest paradox of our time is that we all know our 'system' of government is broken, and yet not a single proposal, from any faction, has earnestly been made to fix the *system.*"

The Professor paused for a long moment, fully aware that no one had any idea where he was going.

"We've all been taught in our system of government that elections are our opportunity to change things—to right our course. But, today, it is the election process itself that is at the heart of our problem. Our electoral process has been compromised, corrupted to the point that no election can effect substantive change... The truth is, elections today reinforce control, not create an opportunity for change. The system will not tolerate substantive change, and we have seen that reality play out daily for many years now. Through the Obama Administration, the Trump Administration and now into the Biden Administration, both sides have tried valiantly to lead, but with almost nothing lasting to show for their efforts. And it would not have mattered in the least if anyone else had been elected. The problem and the present reality would still persist. The *system* is broken, and until we fix the *system,* we cannot change the trajectory of our decent."

"The problems we are facing today have been a long time coming. Almost from the beginning, the rich and powerful have used and manipulated our government to their own benefit. Now, do not misunderstand me. This is not an indictment of the rich. They embody the American dream and have for centuries. Nor is this an indictment of financial success or capitalism. This is purely a focused accusation against those who would use our government for their own benefit at the expense of the people."

"Our Founding Fathers had to wheel and deal to get the support necessary to ratify our Constitution, and, for all its good, we ended-up with a document without adequate real-world controls—specifically, controls on those who would abuse the system for their own benefit. The Founding Fathers were essentially good men, but it did not take long for lesser men to take advantage of what had been left out. As a result, American history is a long narrative of corrupt politicians, land speculators, war profiteers, public works contractors, military contractors, and many, many others who have used government for their own benefit. The truth is that our system of government was always ripe for corruption, and powerful elites have been stealing from us since the beginning."

"It's natural to ask then, why has our *system* survived so long, if it is so corrupt? Because, for most of our history, *We the People* have lived up to the responsibilities as citizens that our Founding Fathers intended, and we have been far more important to our nation's success than our government. The incredible wealth and opportunity that our nation provided spawned patriotism and loyalty unsurpassed in the history of the world, and we have shared a collective belief in the ultimate power of the people. All of these things allowed us to prosper in spite of the serious flaws in our government. We were always responsible for what was happening, and we have always known about it. But we have always been, except for a few remarkable moments in our history, just too comfortable and pleased with ourselves to do much about it."

"Today, as we have discussed, we're in real trouble. We're at the end of our rope, and our systemic problems are threatening to destroy us all. As it was in ancient Rome, most Americans can't comprehend our way of life coming to an end, can't imagine violence or lawlessness on a massive scale… but it is coming. And the chaos that will form in its wake has the potential to be no less debasing to the world than the Dark Ages were to the collapse of Rome."

"We've all heard a lot about the 'Establishment' in the last few years. It is very real. Although, it means dramatically different things to different people. For me, it is simply those who would use our government for their own benefit—putting their personal interests above the greater good of the people. Certainly, that would include anyone who would employ a lobbyist; anyone who would hire someone who formerly worked in government to help them gain and maintain government contracts or favors; anyone who would operate a Political Action Committee or Super PAC; anyone who would contribute a large amount of money to the electoral process—in particular those who would contribute millions or tens of millions of dollars; and of course, the armies of political operatives, both in and out of government, who are willing to do anything for money or power. It's probably also prudent to include foreign governments, trans-national corporations and super rich non-citizens. And, what's really great," said the Professor with dripping sarcasm. "Because of our incredibly lax laws on political corruption, well-intended attempts to control campaign spending that went bad and a list of court cases that undermined everything, the overwhelming majority of actual government corruption is completely legal today. And why wouldn't it be? It's the Establishment and their willing servants in Congress who wrote the laws."

"But, again, we've been aware of all of this for a long time… For years now, every new campaign calls for change, and yet everyone who finds success must first fall in line with the Establishment cartels. Consider what it takes to get elected to office. Say you're an honorable person, who wants to work for good government. The cost of running for Congress has gone from a few thousand dollars, when I was a kid, to tens-of-millions or even hundreds-of-millions of dollars today. To start, you may contact a handful of Political Action Committees that support positions with which you strongly agree. No harm, no foul, but that's not enough money to make it work. To get more, you have to go deeper into the Establishment: hire operatives with the right connections; use the money you raise to build more relationships to other PACs and Super PACs; and very soon you are nothing more than the talent—a figurehead in a web of people, entities and lies who want something in return for what they've given you. You may even convince yourself that you are your own person and make your own decisions, but that is nothing more than something you tell yourself so you can sleep at night. Your positions come ready-made from Establishment entities that call the shots—entities that have wildly more power and influence than you do."

"The really scary part of this is how this reality impacts on the foundational nuts and bolts of our republic—the part we think we control. All of these Establishment entities, no matter their respective interests, are managed by zealous operatives who care nothing for the greater good. They are singularly and passionately focused on their own mission, and that emotional connection is exacerbated by the fact that their personal income, status and power derives directly from the interest they serve. No matter if we strongly support and believe in their efforts, we have to ask ourselves, how reasonable do you think these people are willing to be to find workable solutions to our problems? Do they even want to solve problems, or do they want to keep going to work in their posh K

Street offices and living in their beautiful DC estates? We all know what the answer is… It is in their self-interest to maintain the status quo in order to perpetuate their livelihoods, their lifestyles, their power and their uncompromising positions. The Establishment always puts itself first, and that is the fouled gear that broke the system. It is all about money and power, and as virulently as Establishment entities may react to that accusation, every one of us knows that it is the absolute truth."

"Think about how they go about their mission. Every day it seems, they scream *the sky is falling, the sky is falling* for no other purpose than to raise money. There may be a shred of truth in their cries of indignation, or there may not. It is completely irrelevant to their goal. They are mining sound bites and reactions to raise money. Reality, practicality, functionality or genuine democratic solutions are of no interest to them. Their extremist statements have no aspiration to find common ground. Every one of their hyperbolic exhortations is just another gimmick and solving problems for the greater good is not even a consideration. Why do you think these young congressional striplings skip through the halls of Congress throwing hand grenades without any regard for the damage they do to their own party? It is because the money they can raise as a result of their wild-eyed accusations is dramatically more important to them than the hierarchy of their party, their place in Congress or their responsibilities of office. They don't care. Their goal is to raise money, to become famous and the nation be damned."

At this point you could see the faces in the crowd visibly tighten as the Professor spat out his final words with righteous venom. As he had foretold, they were recognizing the truth, and emotion was welling up inside of them. This was going somewhere, and maybe for the first time in their young lives, they were feeling a sense of responsibility.

"In spite of what has happened to us, it is important to note that all along the way good people have tried to do the right thing. With noble intent, Congress tried to write legislation to curb campaign corruption in the early 1970s. McCain-Feingold at the beginning of this century made a valiant bipartisan effort to get things under control, but statutory law has repeatedly proven inadequate to the task. McConnell v. FEC, McCutchen v. FEC and Citizens United v. FEC collectively reinforced a legal footing so profoundly immoral almost any financial manipulation of the system these days is legal. In fairness to stare decisis, the Court's rulings were well reasoned, but their effect has scrapped away every bit of hope we had in reigning in the Establishment's abuse of power. The late Justice John Paul Stevens wrote in his dissent of the Citizens United decision, 'A democracy cannot function effectively when its constituent members believe laws are being bought and sold.' And that is exactly what is happening."

"These rulings have created a legal infrastructure that gives the wide-ranging interests that comprise the Establishment de facto control over our government—a position that our Constitution had reserved for our elected representatives. This new system has allowed these groups to develop immense power based solely on their ability to raise money, and in the last decade or so, has gradually changed our democracy into the oligarchy it is today. Yes, that is what I said, oligarchy. The truth is the American Establishment is a functioning oligarchy in every sense of the definition."

"Just for a moment, let's test our reality. Most of us have neighbors, family and friends with whom we differ politically. I would be willing to wager this robe and my ballcap, in other words, all that I own, that if we sat down with these people we care about, we could design completely fair and workable solutions to any of our problems. There are three reasons why this would work. First, the great majority of the American people are not radically left or right. It's only about ten percent or so on both ends of the political spectrum, who incidentally control the oligarchy, who are the extremists. Most of us, whether Democrat or Republican, are reasonable and fair minded. Second, fund raising dollars would not be our first and last consideration. And third, we truly care about the people with whom we disagree. That, my friends, is how our system was intended to work, and how it does work in small towns and counties throughout this country… Again, most Democrats and most Republicans are fair, reasonable, good people—not at all the frightening caricatures painted by the minions of the Establishment."

"The point is, our *system* of government and our electoral process is working against a functioning democracy, and it will eventually destroy us. If there is no truth, no honor, no integrity—only brash, self-serving conquest, where only the ends-justify-the-means—our days as an American republic are numbered. Both sides play the game. It is dirty. It is unscrupulous, and there are trillions of dollars in play. Destroying someone's life or even ending a few who get in the way is not a fictional element in this saga…"

"When I was a young man, Washington, DC, was a warm and congenial sort of place. There was a sense of awe in seeing it for the first time: monuments to our history and our great leaders; temporary homes of those who were elected by the people to serve; respected institutions of higher learning dotted its backdrop; and at its center, a patriotic cemetery to honor our fallen heroes. It was beautiful… but today, all of those things have been over-grown by a cancer of gaudy opulence, pretension and power… "

"I have done my best today to speak in clear terms and to tell the truth. I have been direct and avoided hyperbole as much as possible. I have used the word oligarchy in its textbook definition and described how it functions—without any sense of virtue—always putting the interests of the few above the many—leadership without humility—operating as a polyanthus of corruption. These United States are currently ruled by an unscrupulous oligarchy that will stop at nothing to control our lives and destroy anyone or anything that gets in its way. This is not at all what it was supposed to be. Today, *We the People* are a joke. *We the People* serve only the interests of the Establishment who serve themselves at the feeding trough of our government and our future…"

As painful a scenario as he had outlined, there was a genuine sense that the Professor had a plan, and for some odd reason faces began to open-up with a shiny optimism. He had them. They were ready for the next step, and he took a long pause to choose his final words carefully.

"As horrible a picture as I have painted for you today," the Professor said, lifting his eyes to the horizon. "I believe there is a way back—a prescription for a full recovery—better than ever. You see, you, right here, have the power to fix it… and I look forward to seeing you all next week to tell you how."

CHAPTER

THREE

AFTER THE MUSIC WANED, the crowd stared at each other for a moment. A few laughs could be heard sparking up from an otherwise quiet and uncertain collective consciousness. They had been slowly brought under the professor's control, fixated on every word and with almost no warning, he was gone. There was almost a sense of panic. They wanted to hear more. This couldn't be over they reasoned with themselves.

Eventually, people began to turn to each other to discuss what they had witnessed. Most found themselves talking to strangers. There was a near universal acceptance that what Professor Fletcher had said was important, and most felt they had witnessed something extraordinary—historic. To many it was an affirmation of what they already knew. To others it provided order to what previously had only been chaos and emotional assumptions, and for some, it was an open and clear call to action. They were frightened by the revelations, but whatever their feelings were individually, no one planned on missing part two.

Johnny and Katie were no exception. They continued to watch in silence as the Professor disappeared from view. Both were deeply moved by the experience and felt the same run of emotions that everyone else was feeling. They had witnessed something they would never forget.

"I wonder what in the hell he has in mind?" said Johnny, finally.

"I don't know, but I feel like I just witnessed Moses warn Ramses to let his people go," responded Katie.

"I know," said Johnny, laughing at the image. "I'm not going to miss the next one."

One of Katie's colleagues leaned in and asked, "Say, we're going over to the *Slowdown*. You wanna come?"

"Sure," she responded.

"You in?" she said, turning to Johnny.

"Ahhh, yeah," responded Johnny. "I'm not sure where that is."

"Just take Cuming down to 14th, take a right and park in back," directed Katie.

"I'll see you there," Johnny said, as they all broke into different directions.

Katie bit her lower lip as she looked after him walking away.

Johnny called Candy as he walked toward his Jeep and explained what he was up to. As he turned onto 14th Street, he was a little surprised to see what appeared to be a very popular nightclub as his destination. He'd envisioned something along the lines of a quiet academic bar, but he quickly realized the *Slowdown* was something more akin to a music-driven hipster retreat. Of course, he wasn't too sure what a hipster retreat was, but it seemed to fit his sense of things. As he was parking and wondering if he was going to feel out of place, he realized that he wasn't the only one who had come from the speech. It was still early by nightclub standards, but the parking lot seemed to be filling up with a long line of cars coming from Creighton.

The group was lucky to find a table by the window. After quick introductions and a drink order, a balding young professor about Katie's age named Curt started the discussion. He was sitting on the other side of Katie, so Johnny, owing to a slight hearing impairment left over from his first combat deployment in Iraq, had to lean forward and cock his head toward him so that he could hear.

"Other than the histrionics of the whole deal," said Curt, smugly. "I seriously doubt if he can follow through."

Melody, a 30ish African American business professor sitting directly across from Katie agreed, "Yeah, I don't see where he goes with this either. I think he'll go down one partisan path or the other. Does anyone know his politics?"

"Typical old white man," responded Cara, an alabaster-skinned women in her late twenties, with tats, bleached, chopped hair and a nose ring. "Likes to hear himself talk."

"No," responded Katie, directly. "I think he's a liberal, but I don't think any of this has been staged this way as a ruse to go partisan. Right now, I'm taking this at face value, and I think most everyone else is too."

"I agree," said Charlie, a matronly woman in her late forties from the Philosophy Department. "I know him about as well as anybody, which isn't well. He's a brilliant and introspective guy. I don't think he'd be doing any of this if he weren't completely serious about it. He's just the kind of person who sees things that others don't… And, for the record, I think he's a conservative."

Johnny sucked in a little air which captured everyone's attention. He was reluctant to chime-in with a group he didn't know, but he followed his breath with an offering, "I like to listen to what people say, as opposed to what I expect. And, from what I know about the Professor, he does his research without bias. He's incredibly clear of thought and very strategic in what he recommends."

"And how do you know the Professor?" asked Curt, with a slightly incredulous edge.

"We met in Afghanistan," said Johnny.

"When he was with the CIA?" said Cara, with a youthful air of supe-riority. "So, you another misogynistic, racist, old white man?"

"Cara, really?" said an annoyed Katie. "Can you at least let him get one beer down before you start your bullshit?"

"No, it's okay," responded Johnny, smiling directly at Cara. "I have been guilty of a lot of things in my life, and I am an old, white man. But I'm more of a Bernie Sanders Progressive." Everyone chuckled at the unexpected twist, including Cara.

"Really?" said Katie, turning in surprise toward Johnny. "I figured a career Army guy, like you, would have a little Prussian bent about you."

"Well, there's certainly some of those fellows around, but there's a surprising number of us forward thinking liberals in the army too," said Johnny. "My family became Nebraska Democrats with William Jennings Bryan. I didn't know Republican was a stand-alone word until I was in graduate school. I always thought it was Goddamn-Republican."

"Alright. I can hang-out with this guy," said Cara, playfully, giving Johnny a high five. "He's on my team. In your face K-T."

Johnny looked quizzically at Katie and asked, "Does that mean you're a Republican?"

Cara jumps in, "Yeahhhh, a mother-fucking—MAGA hat wearing, white supremacist."

"God, you're annoying Cara," said Katie. "Didn't you hear anything Professor Fletcher said tonight? Are you a socialist, bomb-throwing, tear the whole thing down and start over Progressive?"

"Abso-fucking-lutely," said Cara, loudly.

"And who is your PhD advisor?" said Katie, feigning a threat.

Everyone laughed, as Cara looked back at her with a manufactured corkscrew expression on her face.

"Great band tonight." said Charlie, making a joke to intentionally part ways with the discussion.

The first round arrived and discussions shifted to the band and the crowd. There were a lot of students down from the campus, several of them still wearing their robes and caps. Johnny watched the younger crowd carefully and noted to himself that other than the changes in music and style, not much was different from when he was in college.

He couldn't pick it all up, but it sounded like Curt was working very hard to convince Katie she needed to leave with him. Katie wasn't having any of it. As the conversation became more intent, she became more annoyed. The group started to break apart, a couple rolling their eyes as they left the table. After everyone sitting across from them had left, Johnny switched to the other side and turned his legs toward the room—attempting to be as far away from the conversation as possible without being rude.

Just as he was about to offer his apologies and leave, Katie said to him, "Johnny, would you mind dropping me off at my car back on campus?"

Pretending to be completely unaware of their conversation, Johnny responded with a smile, "Sure, no problem. I was just leaving." Without saying goodbye, Katie took Johnny's arm and headed for the door.

Once they were outside, Katie apologized, "Sorry to use you like that, Johnny. I just needed to get away from that asshole."

"No, I'm happy to be of service," said Johnny. "He didn't seem to be willing to take no for an answer."

"As a rule, PhDs are not without ego," said Katie. "But Curt just cannot imagine why anyone would not fall immediately in love with his beautiful mind."

"Not his bald head?" joked Johnny.

"Exactly," laughed Katie, as Johnny helped her into his Jeep.

"How gallant," responded Katie.

"Some vestiges of tradition I just can't get past," said Johnny, as he handed her the seat belt.

Once they got out of the parking lot, Katie opened-up, "I made the mistake of using him for sex not long after I moved here last winter. Since then, he just won't let it go."

"I hate it when that happens," said Johnny, attempting to be funny.

Laughing, Katie said, "Did I shock you?"

"No, not hardly," said Johnny. "When you go on deployments of a year or more at a time with a bunch of guys that have the market cornered on testosterone, you see about everything."

"I imagine," said Katie. "That's got to be hard."

Johnny turned off Cuming Street into campus.

"I'm in that lot over there, white car," she said. "It must have been tough being away from your wife all of that time."

"You get used to it—Facetime, sat. calls," responded Johnny.

As smoothly as possible, Katie reached over and put her hand on Johnny's thigh, and asked, "So, were you ever a bad boy on deployments?"

Johnny pulled up next to her car and stopped. He had been caught completely off-guard and there was that moment of hesitation where he noticed just how stunningly attractive the woman really was. Still, he took a deep breath, moved her hand away, and said, "No. I couldn't do something like that."

Blown completely away and trying not to show her embarrassment, Katie said, awkwardly, "Ah, that's, ah, impressive."

"Nah, not really," said Johnny. "Marriage vows and hopefully my word in general are still pretty solid. Guess I've got my Dad to thank for that."

"How so?" asked Katie, seriously wondering what had set him apart from the predominance of toxic masculinity in her experience.

Johnny chuckled to himself in remembrance, "The night before I got married, my Dad and I were walking down the end-rows of the cornfield by our house. It was springtime, and we were watching one of those crazy beautiful Nebraska sunsets. You know, every color you can imagine just splashed across the sky. He stopped and turned, looked me right in the eye, and said, 'John, Candy may be the most beautiful girl at the University of Nebraska right now, but that time is going to be gone in a slippery second. No matter how that may change or any of a thousand other things change, your commitment tomorrow is your commitment forever. And, if you can hold on to that one simple black and white requirement, everything else in your life will fall into place."

"Wow," said Katie softly. "That's… deep."

"Dad didn't say a whole lot, he was just a Nebraska dirt farmer like his father before him, and he wasn't big on platitudes," said Johnny. "In fact, that may have been the only thing like that he ever said to me, but I never forgot it. If you can hold onto one honest, important commitment in your life, you see everything else with greater clarity."

"That's interesting," said Katie, deep in thought. "So, was it true?"

"Was what true?" responded Johnny.

"Was Candy the most beautiful girl at the University of Nebraska?" said Katie, smiling.

"Oh, yeah, she was," responded Johnny. "She was a cheerleader and big sorority girl—a Theta—way, way out of my league. I think I was in three different classes with her before I had the nerve to say, 'Hello.'"

"So, how did you get together?" asked Katie.

"I was so obsessed, I decided I couldn't risk not being randomly selected to be in another class with her and asked her out for dinner in the spring of our junior year? She was totally taken off guard, couldn't come up with an easy reason why not, and said 'Yes.' Blew me away, didn't quite know what to say. Had to bum money off four different friends to have enough to take her out somewhere special."

"It must have worked," responded Katie.

"No," he said laughing. "It was a disaster. I was so nervous. I couldn't talk. I was an idiot. She couldn't wait to get back to her house."

"So, what happened?" said Katie.

"About a month later, I was at a bar downtown with some friends, and this guy was pushing his girlfriend around. I watched him for a while, and he kept getting more and more aggressive. Eventually, he shoved her up against the wall pretty hard. I didn't know either one of them, but I came across the room fast, grabbed him and pushed him out the back door into the alley. He was bigger than I was, but I didn't care. I was so pissed at what I'd seen, I was gonna kick his ass no matter who he was. Luckily, he was exactly what you expect those kind of guys to be—total coward."

"So, you're a hero too," said Katie.

"Pfft, no. I've known a lot of heroes in my day, and they're all the same," said Johnny. "They're just at the right place at the right time to do what needs to be done. They never think about how it may impact on them. They just commit."

"So, how did that get you together with Candy?"

"I hadn't seen her at the bar, but after the deal was over, she walked up and thanked me. She had a close friend in high school whose father was… abusive, so it was something very personal to her. She asked me to walk her home, and we talked all night."

"That must have been some conversation," said Katie.

"Yeah, I remember practically every word of it," said Johnny. "Things guys and girls don't talk about much when they're young—shared values, honor, character…"

"Johnny, I'm really ashamed about what I did earlier. I wish I had a good excuse," said Katie, shaking her head.

"Nah, don't worry about it," said Johnny. "If it helps, I was totally flattered."

"That's very gracious—exactly what I would expect from you," she responded.

Johnny smiled awkwardly.

"You know my Dad loved my Mom like that I think," said Katie. "We never talked about it. I kind of wish we had…"

Johnny continued to listen in silence.

"Well… this has been one amazing evening," said Katie. "Thank you."

"For what," asked Johnny.

"For introducing me to someone a girl can honestly look up to," she said, smiling.

"Well, I better get home so Candy can put my ego back where it belongs," responded Johnny, smiling.

Katie stuck out her hand and shook his firmly, "Little Johnny Jones it was a genuine pleasure getting to know you a little better tonight. I hope I haven't offended you to the point where we can't do this again?"

"I think next Friday sounds good," responded Johnny.

"Definitely," said Katie, as she climbed out of the Jeep and turned toward her car.

Johnny pulled out of the parking lot and went West on Cuming. Standing next to her car, Katie looked after him and said out-loud to herself, "So, that's what a real man looks like…"

CHAPTER

FOUR

THE SAME REPORTER who had written the story for the *Omaha World-Herald* the week before, covered the July 5th event. This time, he was exceedingly careful to get the story right. In fact, there was no sense of bias of any kind. He was completely accurate and must have recorded the entire speech, as he quoted the Professor perfectly and made sure none of the quotes were taken out of context. What the Professor had said about the press must have hit home with him, and he did his profession very proud by taking up the challenge. He must have also had a long talk with his editor and the editorial board, because the story was front-page news in the Sunday Paper. The follow-up event also received front page attention the day before the second speech, and it was accompanied by an editorial. The paper enthusiastically suggested that everyone who had the opportunity, ought to be there if for no other reason than to witness the fulfillment of what the editorial called, "… the most profound promise of our time."

It was hard to really know what was in their mind at the time, but the Omaha media was distinctly lacking in any kind of cynicism about the second speech. Maybe, it was out of respect to Creighton University or the tone of the *World-Herald's* follow-up story, but the in-town media seemed genuinely curious and hopeful about what was coming in the second speech. The four television stations ran clips of the first speech, reported on background stories and generously promoted the follow-up speech. Local talk radio also ran select clips that supported their general narrative and demonstrated remarkable restraint of opinion in waiting to see exactly what the Professor would say in the coming week. Most commentators had a lot of fun with the caps and robes, and one announced that he would show up in cap and robe himself and broadcast live from the event. As it drew nearer, everyone in the Society of the Robes, as Andy St. John's organizing committee was called, was nervous about the generally positive coverage. It was all too good to be true, and that worried them.

In contrast to the voluminous social media effort that the Society had made to promote the first speech, they decided to soft sell the second. They were concerned that too much media attention outside of Omaha before they were ready could leave them vulnerable. As much as they could, they wanted to be ready for any eventuality. Of course, they understood that control was completely out of their hands, but they at least wanted to do everything they could to consider and reconsider the many possibilities. They were anticipating a national media frenzy after the Professor's second speech, and they needed to be prepared to take it to the next level, no matter what path was revealed. Simply put, they knew it was going to be big, and they wanted to do everything they could to be ready for it.

Given the citywide anticipation, Andy St. John received permission from the administration to hold the speech at Morrison Stadium. Given all of the positive coverage the event was getting, the president and the rest of the board of Creighton University were feeling very supportive. Of course, none of them had any idea what to expect, but like everyone else, they were hopeful that good things might come. Like the students, they reasoned the event might become something Creighton would be very proud of one day. One thing was for sure, Andy St. John knew how to sell it. He told them that the Professor's second speech was going to become one of the most important speeches in American history and that Creighton University would forever be mentioned in the same sentence. He said it with enough conviction that they believed he believed it was true, and that was good enough for them.

The origin of the organizing committee and Andy's leadership of it began after one of the Professor's more passionate lectures that past spring. It had been a mic dropper, as they say, and Andy invited a group of male and female classmates to discuss whether the Professor's ideas made any sense in the real world. Could something like that really be done? In their youthful exuberance, they decided it was worth a shot. From there, they encouraged the Professor to conceive a serious and practical plan for his ideas to be realized—a plan for the people to take the country back from the Establishment. In the beginning, it was all just fun and games—a college romp. But, after several weeks of consideration, the Professor came up with something quite unexpected that changed everything.

One evening they met in one of the university's old conference rooms—cloistered, shadowy, historic and reverent. Step-by-step the Professor laid out the plan to them speaking almost in a whisper. The group listened intently. He spoke for almost two hours, but to them it seemed only a few moments that they didn't want to end. It was so accessible and vivid, such a clear vision of what was possible, and with each step, the group began to genuinely believe it could all be done, just as described. Of the twelve that were there for the presentation, every one of them moved into a frame of mind that would most accurately be described as obsession. To a person, six young men and six young women, what had once been a lark was now a revolution in the making—for the sake of their generation and their nation.

At the recommendation of the Professor, they used the successes of the Revolutions of 1848 and the Arab Spring as models, and their failures as a warning. As they worked toward their goal, the group became deadly serious. They reasoned that these were ideas that could change the world, but without a carefully played hand, it could just as easily end in failure and destroy lives. Though the Professor was a material partner, he was not a player in their planning or their execution. He had a pretty good idea of what was happening but understood this had to be their play.

Outwardly, by the time of the first speech, the group was calling themselves the "Society of Robes," a lighthearted reference to the bathrobes they wore. Privately, however, they were calling themselves the "Society of Robespierre," a homage to a much more intense and ambitious spirit. Behind the irreverence, humor and carefully crafted image of a fun-loving group of Gen Z's out on a lark, was in fact a well-organized and passionate group of revolutionaries with a strategic plan and a deep commitment to change the world. Andy was a natural leader who understood how to build a vision and use drama to create passion. Later, some would say it was a terribly dangerous combination of things to put in the hands of a bunch of kids. To that, the Professor would respond to a *Washington Post* reporter, "Alexander the Great was 20 when he became King of Macedonia; Elizabeth I was 25 when she became Queen of England; and Napoleon was 24 when he won the Siege of Toulon, and the list of remarkable youth in history goes on. Only a fool would have underestimated those kids."

CHAPTER
FIVE

ON FRIDAY MORNING, Katie called Johnny to confirm that he was going to attend the Professor's final speech. Assuming she had Johnny's cell phone number, she was caught off guard when Candy answered.

"Hey," she said. "This is Katie. How are you?"

"Absolutely wonderful," responded Candy. "I've been in the garden all morning. The mourning doves are singing in the sunshine, and it is just gorgeous. God has got to be from Nebraska."

"Must be," said Katie, chuckling. "I've been grading summer school mid-terms, fueled by six cups of coffee—not a beautiful sight… Say, is Johnny around? I want to make sure he's going to the Professor's speech tonight."

"Oh, I'm sure he is. He had such an interesting night last time," replied Candy, with an ever so slight hint of knowing.

"Yes, it was fascinating," said Katie, her neck and face flushing. She went blank, grasping for something to say.

Candy bailed her out, "He's not here right now, but I'll have him call you as soon as he comes in."

"Thanks, I appreciate it," said Katie, and abruptly hit disconnect. "Fuck," she said to herself.

Katie had been thinking a great deal about what had transpired between the two of them the previous week. It was terribly embarrassing, but it led her to a lot of self-examination. Everything about her life had always been filled with crazy contradictions. She was smart and well-educated enough to understand she had problems. She had a good idea about how to solve them but was never quite capable of following through. She'd tried counseling a half dozen times but found the experiences annoyingly predictable. An absent mother, alcoholic father, feudal Irish family, archaic and contradictory teachings of the church—she knew the excuses and the programmed responses cold, but none of them satisfied her own sense of responsibility. It was only a matter of discipline, she told herself. She wanted to be a better person but didn't have what it took to change. Maybe Johnny did, she thought, but that's a lot to lay on somebody. *Oh God, I'm a mess,* she said to herself and started reading her papers again.

She'd only read a few lines when the phone rang, startling her. It was Johnny. She answered, "Hey, what cha do'in?"

"Oh, just cutting-back a few weeds," he replied.

"Yeah, me too. Grading midterms," said Katie, making a weak joke. "Say, I wanted to make sure you were going to the speech tonight."

"Absolutely, it appears to be the hot ticket," said Johnny.

"Literally," responded Katie. "It's like a thousand degrees outside."

"Nah, it's just good summer weather," he responded. "Maybe the evening breeze will cool things off by speech time."

"Gah, I hope so... Say Johnny, I was wondering if you would be willing to go to dinner with me after the speech," said Katie, intentionally rushing into the next sentence so she could explain. "I was hoping you could, maybe, help me... I think I could use a big brother."

There was a brief hesitation. "Sure," Johnny said, in a comforting tone. "I'd be glad to."

"Thanks," said Katie, feeling uncharacteristically vulnerable. "Why don't you meet me in the same lot you dropped me off last week. I'll get you a pass, and we can walk from there."

"Sure," said Johnny.

"We should probably get there earlier this week," said Katie. "Everyone's saying, it's going to be crazy."

"What are you thinking," asked Johnny.

"I'm thinking at least an hour early," replied Katie.

"Yeah, that's a plan," said Johnny. "I'll see you about seven."

"Good, and ah… thanks," said Katie.

"Sure," replied Johnny, cheerfully, and they disconnected.

Due to the extensive media coverage, everybody in town was talking about the speech even if they weren't planning to be there. What was it about? Who was this professor? What's Creighton got to do with it? Was it all just an elaborate joke? Lots of questions and not many answers. It was almost impossible not to overhear conversations about it at restaurants, bars and convenience stores all around town. Creighton administrators were in daily conversations with Campus Security, the Omaha Police Department and the Omaha Fire Department making sure everything that could be anticipated was. Extra port-o-potties were ordered, an aide station was set up at the stadium and metal detectors and screening lines were organized. As an added precaution, the Police Department strategically deployed their SWAT team nearby and held a large number of officers in riot gear on campus. No one knew exactly what to expect, but this was a political event in dangerous times. Everyone wanted to be ready for anything.

CHAPTER
SIX

THE HEAT HAD NOT LET UP by seven o'clock, and the Jeep's open top and open doors didn't help much as Johnny took the same route he had taken the week before. He'd been in the sun all day, and even though he showered and changed, he felt a steady stream of sweat pouring down his back.

As he drove near campus, cars were already starting to fill every available parking spot in the area. Even the empty lots that were used only for ball games were quickly filling to capacity. The general mood seemed festive as if people were going to a game, but there was definitely a charge in the air. Fortunately, the faculty lot that Katie recommended still had several open spots. Johnny saw her car and backed-in next to her.

"We better get moving," said Katie, starting to walk before Johnny even climbed down from his Jeep. "This is nuts. I've never seen so many people on campus."

"Let's go," said Johnny, trotting to catch up.

As they came closer to the stadium, they could see people coming from every direction. The capacity of the stadium was about 6,000 people, but it seemed to them that the crowd would soon be well over that number. After they made their way through the metal detectors and through the covered stands the seating was already filled to capacity. People were gathering on the field in front of the stage.

The Society had a stage erected in the center of the field big enough for a rock concert. On both sides of it were huge video screens so that the crowd in the stands could see clearly. Beneath the screens and on their outside edges were large banks of speakers. They obviously did not want anyone to miss what was being said. In fact, the entire sound system was far more professionally mounted than anyone would have believed necessary. In addition, there were fixed video cameras in front of the stage on both sides and at least three portable cameras moving through the event recording what was happening. All of it added to the anticipation.

Johnny and Katie decided to position themselves on the right flank of the crowd on the field—close enough to see everything that was happening but removed enough from the center of things to be a little less vulnerable. Neither of them had any sense of danger, but then neither of them had any sense of what to expect. Instinctively, both felt more comfortable being cautious.

By the time they found a good place to watch, they estimated the crowd at over 8,000 and growing. Pockets of students in bathrobes and caps were noticeable and seemed to be getting a lot of attention. There were several large groups of veterans, many carrying American flags. The overwhelming majority of those in attendance were clearly students under 30, but there were also a large number of what seemed to be average Nebraskans. There were parents and small kids, and in most respects, other than the pockets of student and veteran groups, it all looked much like any other mid-summer night's gathering. There was considerable apprehension on the part of the members of the Society, but there didn't seem to be anything negative going on. In general, you'd have to say the crowd was just having fun.

The speech did not begin at 8 o'clock as planned. It was clear there were many people still filtering in, and evidently, a determination had been made to wait. However, after twenty minutes, the music that had been playing stopped, and Father Hendrickson, President of Creighton University, unexpectedly walked to center stage. By that time, people had filled-in the space between the stands and the stage. Later it was revealed that over 12,000 people were inside the stadium and about half that on the outside.

Father Hendrickson stood before the microphone, seemingly filled with pride, and said, "I would like to welcome everyone to Creighton University this evening. We are very pleased you have joined us and hope you have a memorable evening."

With that, he made the sign of the Cross and said, "In the name of the Father, and the Son, and Holy Spirit." About half of the crowd joined in crossing themselves.

Then he said, in a particularly impassioned voice, "Dear Heavenly Father, grant us wisdom and hearts filled with love, that we may learn and grow together, and project dignity and gratitude in all that we do. All this we pray through our Lord Jesus Christ, your son, who lives and reigns with you in the unity of the Holy Spirit, one God for ever and ever. Amen. In the name of the Father, and the Son, and the Holy Spirit."

For some peculiar reason, after his invocation, there seemed to be a sense of calm that fell immediately over the crowd. There had not been any discernable tension or apprehension before, but after Father spoke it was different—like the sweet calm after a summer rain.

The Professor had been walking inconspicuously around the North edge of the crowd, across the artificial turf toward the stage when the prayer began. He stopped, crossed himself with the others, bowed his head and then continued walking when it ended. A smooth and powerful melody began to rise again from the banks of speakers. It was Josh Groban singing the prayer song, *Bring Him Home* from *Les Misérables*. As the song played, the lyrics flashed across the two video screens and without prompt the crowd began to sing along. As sweat poured down their arms and necks, thousands became invested in the song and the growing emotion of the event. It had been planned to elicit an emotional response, but no one expected it to be quite so moving. As the song came to a close, *Bring Him Home... Bring Him Home...*, the crowd's voices drifted to silence and the Professor walked with a slight limp to center front. A huge roar of applause startled him, as it did the members of the Society in their varying perspectives around the stadium. Smiles and expressions of deep pride draped across their faces.

Speech 2: Carpe Diem

The Professor looked for a moment across the mostly youthful crowd with a single tear running down his face. Like Jean Valjean, his love for these young idealists was profound. Andy picked the song with the intent of moving both the crowd and the speaker, and as everything else that day, it worked beyond his expectations. The people were listening.

"Thank you, thank you all," began the Professor. "I had not expected that song to be played tonight, but it is stunningly appropriate. After all, what we are about is a very old story. The struggle of common people against tyranny and corruption is as old as mankind, and its cost has left millions upon millions of parents in sorrow through the ages… Some of you may be thinking that I am being overly dramatic. I assure you I am not. Where do you think it ends, when a people no longer trust their leaders or their government? Where do you think it ends, when two equal factions of a society no longer trust each other? Where do you think it ends, when both sides absolutely believe that they exclusively own the moral imperative? Where do you think it ends, when more money than any of us can dream stands in the balance? And where do you think it ends when either side is willing to do absolutely anything for power?"

"The answer to these questions comes in thousands of boys and girls charging across open fields with bullets and bombs cutting them down in mass, or by standing a barricade, as in *Les Misérables*, praying to God that their mothers can find their bodies in the morning sun. No, I am not being overly dramatic. When a people can no longer find common ground, common purpose, the lessons of history are all too clear. It ends in killing fields of anger and hate."

"But I believe there is a way forward that does not end in the horror of civil war, and that is why we are here. There is still a path back to democracy. Though it has been largely ignored, our Founding Fathers left us a clear blueprint, and our own history has prepared us for peaceful revolution. There is a way to fix it—fix it all… But to succeed, there are several things we must do together."

"First, we have to jettison our hatred and open our hearts again to virtue. That does not mean we have to start trusting immediately. What it means is that we have to first demand virtue of ourselves and live in the whole truth. Then, we will have to start trying to see into the hearts and minds of those with whom we disagree and try to understand the foundation of what they believe. If we can go that far, we can start rebuilding our trust.

"Second, to succeed our vision must be capable of convincing the overwhelming majority of Americans to follow us—not just 50 percent, but 70, 80 percent or more. That means we cannot be about petty partisan or ideological goals, no matter how much we believe in them, but instead focus on the fundamental requirements of our republic— tenets on which we all agree. If we can accomplish this, we will find a vast and level field of common ground on which to build."

"Third, we must craft a vehicle, a message, that is simple, clear and direct—something around which we can rally… If we can allow ourselves to be guided by these three principles, we can do this. As God as my witness, we can do this, and bring about a rebirth of democracy in the United States of America!"

"However, there is one more thing, maybe the most important thing, that we will have to do before we can make this work. We will have to conqueror the fear that we are just too small, too insignificant to take on the Establishment. We will have to reign-in our preconceptions of what is possible. If we can do that, our creativity will shine through, and we will make the amazing happen. Let me reassure you. We have all of the power we need. I'll talk more about that later, but for now start expanding what you believe is possible."

"So, let's review our core problems—the things we need to fix: First, as a people and as a government, we've lost our virtue, our truth, and as a result, there is no trust. Second, our elected representatives no longer serve the people. They serve the Establishment that gets them elected. Third, the Establishment is driven solely by an insatiable thirst for power and financial gain."

"Step one, to correct these failures and in the doing fix our system of government, we must begin with a legal foundation, and to do that we need look no further than the *Declaration of Independence.* You see our Founding Fathers anticipated just such a situation as we are in right now. They understood human weakness and the creeping influences of corruption. So, Jefferson included this amazingly relevant passage."

"To secure our rights, Governments are instituted among Men, deriving their just powers from the consent of the governed,—That whenever any Form of Government becomes destructive of these ends, it is the Right of the People to alter or to abolish it, and to institute new Government, laying its foundation on such principles and organizing its powers in such form, as to them shall seem the most likely to effect their Safety and Happiness."

"We've heard those words over and over since we were children. Now, it's time to apply them as they were intended. It is clear to at least 90 percent of us that our system of government is broken. Therefore, it is our legal and God given right to alter our present system and create one that will work in our best interests."

"So, here we go… As I told you from the very beginning, the solution to our problem is nothing special. As a matter of fact, you have said it yourself, and you've heard it many, many times from other people. The truth is that all 90 percent of us who think the system is broken, know exactly why it's broken… It is simple. We need to take the money out of politics. In fact, the only people who don't want to take the money out of politics, are the ones getting rich from it… Now, before you scoff at the idea and tell me why it can't be done, let me tell you exactly how and why it can be done. And, let me remind you, what I said earlier. You are going to have to control your preconceptions. This is the first big test."

"Our government is based on laws, and these laws create the *system.* Our system is broken, so we need to change the laws to fix the system. However, statutory law cannot fix the problem. It has repeatedly been tried and failed—probably even made the situation worse. To fix our system we need a Constitutional Amendment to override all of those Supreme Court cases aligned against us… I can already hear those preconceptions ringing like a pinball machine, so stop. Keep an open mind... There is a way. It can be done, and we can start the whole deal, right here, right now by simply convincing 33 Nebraska State Senators to ratify our amendment."

"Now, don't freak-out. I'll answer all of your questions, one-by-one, but let's start by introducing this hypothetical. What if, we can write an amendment so dramatically straight-forward that almost every one of us agrees it should be ratified. Then, we take this wildly popular Amendment, and we ratify it in the Nebraska Unicameral with the affirmative vote of only 33 State Senators. Without question, the audacity of the move would light up our prairie sky with a media frenzy we can only imagine. Overnight, state legislators and governors nationwide would be thrust into the debate. Hundreds of millions of Americans will have already read and reread the Amendment on every media platform out there. By sheer weight of its honesty and popular support, state legislatures across the nation follow Nebraska in ratifying the Amendment, and before anyone can spell "Establishment," the requisite 38 states have voted for ratification. Some even go so far as to call special sessions to satisfy the will of the people. Slow to catch up, the Establishment files suit to challenge the amendment on the grounds that the requirements of Article V have not been met, but the will of the people is clear. The Supreme Court declares the Amendment valid. It becomes law and our nation is saved."

When the Professor paused, the crowd was so quiet that only the ambient sounds of the city in the distance could be heard. The crowd collectively furrowed their brow and waited in silence for more explanation.

"Let me explain what I call the *Nebraska Strategy*... Article V of the Constitution of the United States says that two-thirds of both houses of Congress or a two-thirds majority of a States Convention are required to propose amendments to the Constitution. Actually, the word 'required' or anything like it does not appear in Article V, and legal scholars for many years have argued that there are other methods of introducing

amendments to the Constitution available to the will of the people—
other methods like the *Nebraska Strategy*. Further, scholars point out
that the Founding Fathers themselves used the same logic to ratify our
Constitution in the first place. They bypassed the procedures established
by the *Articles of Confederation* and succeeded in ratification through
the popular support of the people—exactly what we are planning to do."

"Use your common-sense. We're talking about the will of the people,
and what do you think would more clearly establish the will of the
people—535 men and women in Congress who are largely owned by the
Establishment elite, or 7,383 state legislators who are in every practical
way closer to the people? What's more, there is precedent. According to
the National Archives, 'In the past, State Legislatures have not waited to
receive official notice before taking action on a proposed amendment.
They have either supported or rejected amendments before ever having
been proposed, and their actions have stood. The bottom line is that
in Article V of the Constitution, State Legislatures are singled-out as
dominate. They and only they can ratify amendments to the Constitution. When three-fourths of them agree, an amendment becomes law.
Period."

The crowd continued to remain silent.

"So, let me describe our idea for an amendment…"

Expressions in the crowd were visibly open to what was coming—as
if they intrinsically understood that everything rested on what they were
about to hear. *Here we go*, they repeated to themselves.

"First, we call our amendment, what we propose to be the 28th
Amendment to the Constitution of the United States, *the New Democracy Amendment*," said the Professor. "Because our amendment will
bring about the next step in the evolution of our democratic republic
by elevating the power of the people over that of the Establishment."

> "**Section 1.** *It shall be the duty of the people, the media, and
> the government of the United States to live in the spirit of
> the twelve common virtues of citizenship. These virtues are:*

Truth as the path to understanding; Faith in the goodness
of humankind; Sacrifice for the greater good; Frugality in
the avoidance of waste; Balance to avoid the corruption of
extremes; Discipline to search for excellence; Diligence in
overcoming adversity; Civility in the preservation of unity;
Justice in demonstrating equality under the law; Humility
in the control of pride; Courage to stand alone for right; and
the Honor to live on principle, even in the face of solitude."

"I'm sure many of you were expecting something more profound, and we certainly went around and around about it ourselves. After all, just writing words down on paper is not going to instantaneously make people act right. What we finally decided is that while all of these things were clearly in the minds and the writings of our Founding Fathers, there was nowhere in the Founding documents where they were clearly spelled out. Of course, the *Federalist Papers* include these concepts in context, but nowhere are they written in clear and concise terms for their own sake. Nowhere does it say, if we don't live on principle, democracy can't work. Section 1 does that. And, yes, there are other virtues, like patience, that could have been included, but we believe these twelve capture the essence of the virtues required for democracy to function. We will see how judges apply this section to their rulings. Maybe, it will have little if any impact. After all, most of these concepts are part of the law already, but maybe, just maybe, it will give judges pause to consider a deeper requirement of the law. In any event, we decided that having these virtues clearly spelled-out as a Constitutional duty of the media, the government and the people certainly would do us no harm."

"**Section 2:** *No financial or organizational support,*
whatsoever, shall move from any organization, interest
group, union, or business interest of any kind to support or
oppose any candidate for local, state, or federal office. All
money contributed to local, state or federal campaigns for

office shall be contributed solely by individual donors with a permanent residence within the specific geographic area to be represented and shall be deposited directly to a respective candidate's campaign committee. No contribution, including those made by the candidate, shall exceed $2,000 in a primary election and $2,000 in a general election."

Shouts of dramatic approval rang out as people started nodding in unison to each new feature of the Amendment.

"All campaign contributions must be drawn from personal assets and be publicly recorded with the appropriate oversight body within twenty-four hours of the contribution. The record shall include the date and time, donor's name and address, and the amount contributed.

"In Section 2," the Professor went on. "We go after the money in a very direct way. If you contribute to a campaign: you are limited to how much you can give; you can't contribute out of the geographic area in which you live; and just because you are wealthy does not mean you can exceed the spending limits in your own campaign. No more campaign contributions from political parties. No more campaign contributions from political action committees, or Super-PACs. No more contributions from special interest groups or dark money, and just because you are rich, does not mean you can take advantage of the electoral process."

A passionate ovation and arrant cheers rose from the crowd, and then pockets of people started to get really excited, thrusting their arms in the air and shouting "Yes" and a dozen other exaltations of support. The euphoria grew. This was something that made sense to everyone. The Professor continued.

"Section 3: *All persons employed by the government of the United States, including those serving in elected, appointed, or military positions, shall receive no gifts, compensation,*

*employment, promises of employment, or any other
incentive from companies, individuals, or countries doing
business with the government of the United States. This
prohibition shall continue for a term of two years after the
employee, or elected, appointed, or military personnel, leaves
government service."*

Cheers rose even louder than before, and smiles and laughter exploded on the faces of almost everyone in the crowd. Even the conservative Board Members and College Administrators expressed their approval. The cheering did not immediately subside, but the Professor interrupted to continue.

"Section 4: *All organizations, interest groups, unions,
business interests, or individuals desirous of influencing the
laws and policies of the United States shall be strictly limited
to providing written information to the various government
entities."*

"With Section 4, the definition of lobbyist will change from 'a boil on the butt of our governmental process' to a group of respected academics gathering and publishing information for the good of the union. No longer will lobbying be a corrupt haven for former politicians and military brass looking to exploit the people."

Wild applause and cheers continued to build, and a spontaneous cheer began to form: "U–S–A, U–S–A, U–S–A…" The Professor waited, but again, the roar of the crowd did not subside.

Finally, he broke in again, "Democracy is not a pure thing," he began and waited. "It is based on the premise that people have a say in their future. It presupposes fairness and makes decisions primarily on the basis of the greater good. Along the way, democracies learned that certain individual rights had to be championed in the name of that fairness, and democracy evolved. Even so, it is and always has been a constant struggle to get it right. During the Golden Age of Athens, there was a continual fight against greed and oligarchy, as it was in Rome and as it has been in every nation ruled by democracy through the centuries. What the *New Democracy Amendment* is intended to do is to make it constitutionally unlawful for individuals or groups of powerful people to bend the system to their will. Simply put, it changes the system to make it more democratic while leaving the basic structure envisioned by the Founding Fathers fully intact. It will be the first time in history where the rich and powerful of our nation, those who control the oligarchy under which we live, are constitutionally prohibited from leveraging their economic power over the will of the people."

"The promise of this effort is beyond any of our imaginations. History has taught us that when people believe they have an equal say in their governance; when they believe their government is protecting their interests; and when they believe they have complete freedom to succeed or fail on their own merit, absolutely amazing things can happen. Athens created the foundation of Western Civilization. Rome built the greatest empire of the ancient world. Great Britain created an empire where the sun never set, and the United States of America created a superpower the likes the world has never known. While all are unquestionably imperfect, it is fundamentally clear that the more a government supports the will of the people, the more potential there is for human achievement."

"Nothing like this has ever been attempted. That scares the hell out of people, but our uncertain future should scare them a lot more. Our second American Revolution will be fought with revolutionary ideas, common sense and once again, backed by the dreams of the people. But, to accomplish the task before us, we must begin by thinking about our future and not our past. The old system is corrupt, and we should not judge the path to our future by the broken roads of our past. We have to stop the blame game and making assumptions based on old paradigms. When we take away the ability for the Establishment to use their money and power to corrupt the system, then we can look to our future with optimism. Once again, we can be proud of our nation and trust our leaders, our government and each other."

"We believe that ratification of the *New Democracy Amendment* will change the outlook of America. The people and their representatives will begin to make better choices based on a renewed idealism, and the people will slowly end their apathy and rekindle their passion and commitment to their nation and each other. Representatives will start to make decisions based on their own good conscience and the needs of the people over the self-serving desires of their overseers. Extremist voices will gradually grow quiet, as the mainstream of America reemerges to take its rightful place, and the media denied the current political excess, will look to the horizon and reinstitute their idealism and sacred duty. The profile of politics in America will recede, and the quiet and thoughtful system our Founding Fathers intended will breed political decisions that make sense for everyone. The dramatic reduction of money in the system will force the political class out of existence. Washington, DC, will return to a quiet collegial city on the Potomac, and the United States of America will be saved for future generations."

"While the worst of the Establishment will no-doubt fight with all they have to stop our effort, it is my firm belief that eventually most will join us. The overwhelming majority of our elected representatives got into politics for the right reasons, and most are driven by unswerving patriotism. Once they see what is possible, they will stand with us. Fundamentally, they want what we want. We all grew up believing in *We the People* and what that represents. As a nation, we have always believed in the twelve common virtues outlined in Section 1 and the fundamental fairness they champion. In the end, very few will be against us."

"Taking this all in, can you imagine, just like ancient Athens and the other great democracies, how that could spur technology, industry, economic development and the arts? Can you imagine this nation without its pessimism and narcissistic outlook? Can you imagine this nation when every child once again believes that they can accomplish anything they can dream? And, before you reject my optimism out-of-hand, what's to stop us from creating another Golden Age or Renaissance right here, right now? Have we learned and created everything there is to learn and create? Have we no achievements before us? We have serious problems, but why can't we do something that has never been done before to solve them? This can be done!" the Professor shouted.

The crowd exploded in cheers and applause, and then rapidly quieted to hear more.

"But understand, we cannot live as we have. We must stop attacking each other and find common ground. We have to find new ways to make things work. We have to discover the whole truth and live by it. We can't allow a mindset forged in the corruption of the past to derail a future that is good and true. The past is not our problem. The future is, and if we want a future for our children and our grandchildren, we have to get this right. We have to be positive, forward looking and be so much better in character than those who will be against us, the choice will be obvious to everyone."

"Above all, we cannot follow this course for personal gain. We must capture the imagination of the people and hold it with hope and opportunity and dreams. Everyone, and I mean you, must step up to do your part, to organize and to recapture the spirit of America. As innocent, naïve and optimistic as this all sounds, it is that simple. We have to be true to each other and the virtues in which we believe."

"We must also understand this will be no easy task. It will require every one of us to pitch in. Make no mistake, this will be a real revolution. Those who have the power, money and influence in our broken system will not give it up without a fight, and what we are about is no less dangerous than what our Founding Fathers contemplated in the summer of 1776. We do not foresee a shooting revolution, but that does not mean those who lead this movement will not be targets. The Establishment will fight with their money and influence to derail and minimize us. They will lie and cheat in every way possible to degrade us. And they will do so for only one reason—they do not want to give up their power. *The New Democracy Amendment* will cause some of the most powerful men and women in the world to lose the power to which they have become accustom. They will do anything to stop us, and all we will have on our side is *We the People*… and the truth… From my perspective, they are hopelessly outnumbered…"

The Professor bowed his head slightly and remained motionless for a moment, as if in prayer. Applause began slowly and grew to a frenzy. This was insane. This was unbelievable. This was a beginning. The speakers began playing "Do You Hear the People Sing" from *Les Misérables*, and everyone joined in singing the words that were simultaneously projected onto the screens.

> *Do you hear the people sing?*
> *Singing the song of angry men?*
> *It is the music of the people*
> *Who will not be slaves again!*
> *When the beating of your heart*
> *Echoes the beating of the drums*
> *There is a life about to start*
> *When tomorrow comes!*
>
> *Will you join in our crusade?*
> *Who will be strong and stand with me?*
> *Somewhere beyond the barricade*
> *Is there a world you long to see?*
>
> *Then join in the fight*
> *That will give you the right to be free!*
>
> *Do you hear the people sing?*
> *Singing the song of angry men?*
> *It is the music of the people*
>
> *Who will not be slaves again!*
> *When the beating of your heart*
> *Echoes the beating of the drums*
> *There is a life about to start*
> *When tomorrow comes!*

No one tried to leave until the last word of the song was sung. At that moment, Elizabeth Grayson, one of the twelve members of the Society of Robes took the microphone at center stage. She was a strikingly beautiful young African American woman, who had just won the National Speech Tournament. She had been chosen by the Society as their primary spokesperson.

As soon as she spoke, she immediately drew everyone's attention. They wanted instructions. They wanted someone to guide them to the next step.

"Now, you understand the secret we've been holding since last spring. Now, you understand our optimism, and you share in our passion. I am Elizabeth Grayson, and I am a member of the Society of the Robes and Chief Spokesperson for the *New Democracy Amendment*. There are a few things we need you to do tonight. So, as soon as you have computer access, log onto *NDAmendment.com*... That's *N–D–Amendment.com*. You'll find videos of the Professor's speeches, a copy of the Amendment and a brief on the *Nebraska Strategy*. Tell us who you are and how you can help make this happen. Give us your contact information. Sign the petition, and buy a ballcap, t-shirt or bumper sticker. To get this started, we need the votes of at least 33 Nebraska State Senators. All 49 would be better. Send the link to absolutely everyone you know and everyone who you think needs to know. Tell them why. Let your passion flow. That's it. We'll be in contact. Just like the Professor said, we're going to fix this. We're going to fix it all."

CHAPTER
SEVEN

AFTER ELIZABETH FINISHED, everyone started to talk at once. People were compelled to express their feelings about what they had just witnessed. They wanted to know they weren't alone. They wanted to know it was real. They wanted to know if it really could happen. There were many opinions and even more questions. About 75 percent of the crowd seemed to rush for the exits—most with a clear intent to do exactly what they had been told to do. They were going to log onto the website and join the revolution.

The other 25 percent pushed toward the stage to directly engage the members of the Society. From what they heard and what they experienced, they anticipated this revolution was going somewhere, and their dreams were pushing them to get in on the ground floor. They wanted a life's memory to share, and in an instant, they were marketing themselves to the Society members as passionately as they knew how.

"I'm great at this."

"I'm great at that."

"Senator Fischer is a friend of my mom's."

"Congressman Bacon is a friend of my dad."

It was a remarkable exaltation. Later, journalists and scholars would surmise it was at this very moment that the revolution was born—the moment when the people began to believe there really was a chance to make things right.

Observing this all from the Southern edge of the crowd, Katie turned to Johnny and said, "I need a beer, internet access and a yellow pad, and not necessarily in that order."

"I'm with you. Let's get out of here," responded Johnny, with a giddy smile.

Moving around the edges of the crowd, Katie and Johnny walked swiftly to the nearest exit with Katie leading the way. Johnny smiled at himself, as he realized he hadn't moved with so much adolescent joy since he jockeyed for a good place in the lunch line in high school. They broke into a trot, as many were, and shuffled up the sidewalk toward the lot where they had parked.

As they moved, they heard dramatic affirmations of the Professor's speech.

"I can't think of a single thing he said tonight that wasn't true. When's the last time you could say that about a speech involving politics?"

"It all makes perfect sense."

"I'm totally on board."

"We have to follow through. Dammit, we have to!"

"I cannot wait to get my bumper sticker."

Katie turned and spoke so Johnny could hear, "Why don't we pop up to my office for a minute and let the parking lot clear?"

"Sounds good. I'd like to take a look at this website—*NDAmendment. com*," responded Johnny.

"Yeah, me too," she agreed.

When they got to her office, Katie pulled up the website on her computer. The art and graphic design conveyed a foundation of substance and patriotism, while emitting just the right level of creativity. It was professional, simple and powerful.

"Look at this," said Katie. "The Professor's speech that he just gave is already up." She printed one of the excerpts that had been graphically framed.

> *The truth is that all ninety percent of us who think the system is broken, knows exactly why it's broken… It's simple. We need to take the money out of politics. In fact, the only people who don't want to take the money out of politics, are the ones getting rich from it…*

"These kids are sharp," followed Johnny. "And they love Victor Hugo. Look at the tag line. 'Absolutely nothing is more powerful than an idea whose time has come.' laid over a Nebraska sunrise. God, that's gorgeous."

"Look at the pull down," said Katie.

- The New Democracy Amendment
- The Nebraska Strategy
- Professor Fletcher—Video 1: Mea Culpa
- Professor Fletcher—Video 2: Carpe Diem
- Text, Mea Culpa
- Text, Carpe Diem
- Sign the Petition
- Media Requests
- Contact Information for all Nebraska State Senators
- Revolution Store

"Look, 'Revolution Store,' crack me up," said Katie. They both laughed out loud. "This is unbelievable. Pull that up."

- New Democracy Amendment Bumper Stickers
- New Democracy Amendment T-Shirts
- New Democracy Amendment Ballcaps
- New Democracy Amendment Coffee Mugs
- Red & White Striped Bathrobes w/New Democracy Amendment Logo
- 5' x 3' Red & White Striped Nylon Flag w/New Democracy Amendment Logo

"Bathrobes! Ha! Great logo, and all with an Amazon quality checkout system," quipped Katie.

"So, this is what a 21st century revolution looks like," said Johnny, shaking his head. "Absolutely amazing."

"I can't imagine the thought that went into this," responded Katie. "God, I wish I had been there."

"It's a little hard to wrap my head around. I'm used to people draping bombs around their bodies to make a point," said Johnny.

"I prefer this way," said Katie without emotion. "Maybe the world will learn something."

"Maybe… if it's really possible," responded Johnny.

"If it isn't, we'll find out sooner than later," said Katie. "Why don't you pull down the petition."

I Support Ratification of the New Democracy Amendment

_____

First Name / Middle Name / Last Name

_____

Address

_____

City / State / Zip Code

_____

Cell Phone / Email

Rate your political leanings: Liberal 1 2 3 4 5 6 7 8 9 10 Conservative

What is your level of commitment? Lowest 1 2 3 4 5 6 7 8 9 10 Highest

What skills do you possess that may help our campaign to ratify the *New Democracy Amendment?*

_____

_____

What contacts do you have who may be helpful in ratifying the *New Democracy Amendment?*

_____

_____

_____

_____

"I'm going to fill it out," said Katie.

A serious expression came over Johnny's face. "I've spent a good deal of my career trying to avoid being put on lists," he said. "If we do this, it will definitely put us on somebody's list."

"No doubt," responded Katie, slipping into thought. "I guess this is kind of serious."

"Might be," said Johnny. "Hard to tell what may happen."

"Most people will sign-up without thinking," said Katie.

"I guess it all boils down to this," said Johnny. "Do you believe this is the right thing to do, regardless of the consequences?"

Katie paused for a long moment thinking it over.

"Yeah, I do," said Katie with conviction. "It feels like history…"

"Yeah… me too," confirmed Johnny.

With that, both of them filled out the petition, and even though brief, the credentials each conveyed in their profile was bound to get someone's attention.

Katie was looking out the window, as Johnny hit "submit."

"It looks like most of the peopled have cleared-out," she said.

"Why don't we head down to the *Upstream* in the Market? An old friend of mine owns the place," said Johnny.

"Sure," said Katie. "Love their bread… and their beer."

"Did you know that Omaha literally means to go against the current?" said Johnny. "And the Omaha tribe got their name from being the 'upstream' people.

"I did not," responded Katie, amused by the irony. "What's the Lakota word for beer?"

"Mnipiga," said Johnny, without dropping a beat.

"You made that up!" she said, laughing.

"I did not," said Johnny. "Mnee–pee–ghah."

"How the fuck?"

"A bunch of us in Afghanistan played around with Lakota as a way to communicate without our counterparts knowing what we were saying," said Johnny. "We weren't always sure of the people we had to work with."

"Well, beer would certainly be a word you would need to know," joked Katie.

"I know, right?" responded Johnny. They headed for the Jeep.

The Upstream was more festive than usual, even for a Friday night. It appeared there were several people there who attended the speech, and conversations could be overheard as those who had been there, related various passages to those who had not. Johnny had reserved one of the quiet back booths near the kitchen.

After they ordered the *mnipiga* of their choice, Katie began. "This all seems kind of weird, now that I've gotten to know you, but I really appreciate you taking the time to talk to me. Whether you know it or not, you gave me a really hard punch in the gut last week. I still haven't recovered."

"That… wasn't my intent," responded Johnny, shyly. "I'm sorry… I didn't mean…"

"No, no, I know you didn't. Honestly, it was one of the nicest things anyone ever did for me," said Katie… "There's been serious holes in my character my whole life. Like I said before, I've got all of the excuses in the book, but I truly want to be a better person. Until you stood up and showed me what true character was, I didn't get it. As I've looked back over my life this week, I don't think I've ever had anyone I could genuinely look up to."

"That's too bad," said Johnny. "My life experience has been just the opposite. My family, my teachers and coaches, the officers I served under, the men I served with, it really was a steady river of people who lived on principle."

"Strange how two Midwesterners growing up not that far from one another could have such completely different character models to follow," she said.

"I don't want you to think that my life has been pure as the driven snow, not at all," said Johnny. "Everyone makes mistakes. It's how you deal with them that's important, how you learn from them."

"I've been thinking about this," said Katie. "There is genuine freedom in having clear moral and ethical boundaries."

"I never thought of it that way, but yeah, it's simpler?" responded Johnny. Feeling somewhat awkward about the question, he went on, "But, didn't you grow-up in the church?"

"Yeah, I know there are many good people in the church, priests and nuns—most of them, but they aren't the ones who showed an interest in me. The little boys get all the media attention, but my experience wasn't that different. I was a classic target. Mom died when I was little, and my Dad was rarely sober enough to remember where he lived. The priests seemed so thoughtful and caring, but they eventually got around to their needs… Along the way, I learned it was easy to get what I wanted just by playing the game. It never even seemed that wrong until recently—when the carnage got personal," said Katie. "Since then, I've been pretty sick of myself."

"I hope you understand how completely heartbreaking it is to hear this," said Johnny. "You seem so together, but just recognizing where you are and where you want to be is a huge step forward."

"It doesn't really feel that way," said Katie.

"I know," said Johnny. "But you're on the right track."

"I convince myself every day that I am a tough and powerful woman, just beating the boys at their own game," responded Katie. "But it's all total bullshit, and it's been bullshit almost my entire life."

"You know Katie," said Johnny. "There's a scared little girl in all of us. Maybe more so in the ones who appear the most confident."

"Even you?" asked Katie.

"Particularly me," responded Johnny. "I think soldiers who have been through the shit understand better than anyone how completely random it all is. Go right. Go left. One guy dies. The other lives. It's all a big mystery. If you spend too much time thinking about it…" He made an open gesture with his hands, conveying that there was no answer.

Katie smiled, "I'm not sure it helps knowing that the person I'm counting on to get me out of this sees it all as kind of hopeless."

Johnny smiled back warmly, and said, "I've cried my tears. If I hadn't, I wouldn't be much help to you."

"Let me explain why last week hit me so hard," said Katie, pausing to draw a long, hard breath. "Last year at Princeton, I was having an affair with one of the older more esteemed professors in my department. Fun and games until everyone became aware of it, including his wife."

"Oops," said Johnny.

"I honestly didn't realize he was that into me," said Katie, shaking and then dropping her head. "Without discussing it with me, he asked his wife for a divorce, thinking we were going to ride off into the sunset together or something. I knew his wife. She seemed like a really strong woman, too… I guess she was. She drove her Volvo into a retaining wall on the New Jersey Turnpike at 100 miles an hour."

"Shit. When exactly was this?" asked Johnny.

"Last Christmas… there's more," continued Katie, her face drawn in obvious pain. "He comes to me later that night, basically falling apart—expects me to be his rock. I very coldly told him it was over, and I never wanted to see him again. So, what's he do? He drives into the same wall at the same speed before all of his wife's wreckage had even been cleared away."

"Jesus," said Johnny, under his breath.

"Anyway, I was lucky. I had a couple of old professors at Creighton who made an over-the-top effort to get me a job here," said Katie. "Probably saved my life."

"It's amazing you can function at all," said Johnny, stoically.

"Then, last Friday, without even a moment's hesitation, I make a serious effort to repeat the same incredibly stupid mistake. Like, what the fuck?" said Katie.

Johnny covered his mouth with his hand and studied Katie's face for what seemed to be a long time. It made her so uncomfortable, she didn't know whether to cry, get up and leave or just collapse. Finally, he broke the silence, "Thank you for trusting me with your story," he said, reassuringly. "That had to be tough."

"Tough? Yeah, I've wanted to tell it to someone for a long time, but I haven't been able to go to confession. I haven't been able to tell any kind of counselor. I don't really have any friends or family to tell—no one." said Katie. "I think, deep down, I just want to be punished."

"I think you've done enough of that yourself," responded Johnny. "After my first combat experience, I was having a pretty hard time. I finally went to see a counselor at Fort Bragg. He was an old guy who served with the 5th Group in Vietnam. He'd been in shit I couldn't even imagine. He told me, most of us grow-up learning to build walls to hide our weaknesses. We get really good at it. In any intense profession, like the military, those walls get very thick and very hard. We even convince ourselves we're not scared, that nothing can hurt us. Then when our walls get to holding back more than they can hold, they spill over. That's where you are now."

"You're talking about PTSD, but my problems are about my lack of morality not PTSD," stated Katie in confusion.

"You grew up in the Catholic Church, where moral discipline was at the heart of everything you were taught," responded Johnny. "You may have rationalized it all as some phony shell game, but that core philosophy is still embedded in you. The fact that you want to quote, 'be a better person,' is a clear indicator that morality is important to you. Right now, that's the gigantic wall at your back. Add the trauma you experienced, and you have a perfect cocktail for PTSD."

"Yeah…" responded Katie, quietly. "Okay."

"So, one thing at a time," he said. "I know a psychiatrist who works with the VA, good guy. I want you to go see him."

"A psychiatrist?" responded Katie. "Wouldn't a psychologist be more appropriate?"

"Maybe, if you found the right one," said Johnny. "I know this guy. He's no nonsense, whip smart and if you need a psychologist, he'll steer you to someone good. Most importantly, I trust him."

"Alright," responded Katie.

"There are four basic strategies I use to get on top of things when I start to feel serious pressure," said Johnny. "It wouldn't hurt you to get started right away."

"Should I take notes," asked Katie, smiling.

"I'll send you an email," responded Johnny, without humor. "Meditation is key. Spend some time every day ordering your mind. I call it prayer. I don't know what that looks like for you. You'll have to decided. It might be a good time for you to find a priest you can trust. Maybe, it's time to get right with your faith too. Second, it looks like you already workout some."

"Yeah, since this all happened, I've become kind of a treadmill freak," responded Katie.

"Good, keep it up," said Johnny. "Those endorphins are pure magic. Third, this may seem a little foo-foo, but go to a health food store and get some essential oils or scents for your home and office. I used to burn sage in my office. Be careful of that one though. It smells like weed."

"Seriously?" asked Katie, incredulously.

"I know, but I'm not kidding. Lavender and peppermint are good. Candy used to rub lavender oil on my back and legs at night—really helped me sleep. And I'd suck on peppermint if I was feeling agitated. It all helped," said Johnny.

"Alright," said Katie.

"Fourth, find a way to express yourself artistically. Write, paint, sketch, sculpt—something. I started writing about my experiences. It may have helped more than anything else I did. You don't have to show anyone what you do but do something. It works," said Johnny. He paused for a moment… "I hadn't thought about it before, but I wonder if the Professor's ideas grew out of coping with his PTSD."

"Makes sense," responded Katie.

"They say getting a pet helps too," said Johnny. "You may want to think about it."

"Maybe," said Katie, her eyes lighting up. "The house seems awfully empty when I get home, and I always wanted a dog."

By this time, Katie was feeling a strange sensation. It was an uncommonly warm and pleasant feeling. She thought to herself, maybe this is what trust feels like.

"As to your moral equation," said Johnny, furrowing his brow. "That's the easy part."

"Oh, right," responded Katie, incredulously.

"You've been conflicted almost your entire life over these issues, yes?" asked Johnny.

"Yes," responded Katie.

"So, there is not a lack of definition?" asked Johnny. "You know right from wrong."

Thinking for a moment, Katie replied, "Yeah, I've always been clear about what was right and what was wrong. Wrong just seemed, I don't know, more exciting."

"Until you realize the hidden costs are more expensive than just doing the right thing in the first place," responded Johnny. "And now, you've been made aware. You've reached out for help, and you're ready for change that makes sense."

Tearing-up, Katie replied, "Yeah."

"Good," said Johnny. "Now for your personal support system…"

"My personal support system?" repeated Katie.

"From now on, I want you to look at me, literally, as your big brother. Whenever you feel you're faced with a conflict, call me, anytime day or night. Anytime you're feeling alone or lost, you're more than welcome at our home. Stay as long as you like."

"What about Candy?" asked Katie. "Won't this be weird?"

"She'll be completely onboard," replied Johnny, confidently. "That's who she is. I'm hoping the two of you will become close friends. She won't judge and will probably be better for you than me."

"Sounds too good to be true," responded Katie. "You're not like a cult leader, are you?"

Johnny smiled thoughtfully and said, "There won't be anything easy about this. It will be strange and uncomfortable at first, but you'll have the support you need."

"I don't know what to say," said Katie.

"You're the one doing the work," said Johnny. "We're just adopting you, giving you a family. You'll be expected to do your part too. Join us on all the holidays. You'll like the kids, when you meet them. They're all totally different, fun and full of love. You'll meet the extended family too. They're an interesting lot, pioneer heritage, hard-working down on the farm types who revel in the simple things. They're not exactly a sophisticated group, but I also have a remarkable number of cousins who are professors, army officers, CEOs and even a former ambassador. You'll fit right in."

"Sounds like quite a family," responded Katie, chuckling. Then, after a long moment of reflection, tears began to run down her face. She reached up and wiped them away self-consciously. Johnny remained silent.

Finally, Katie responded quietly, "I ahh… I can't even describe all the feelings that are running through me right now."

"Sure," said Johnny, reassuringly.

"This will take some time to process," said Katie. "But thank you."

Johnny nodded, "Another round?"

"Absolutely," she responded, laughing through her tears.

Conversation returned to a discussion of the Amendment and speculation about how things would move forward from there. After dinner, they were enjoying a root beer float when both of their phones alerted with incoming texts.

Katie read aloud, "Please attend an organizational meeting of the New Democracy Amendment Organizational Committee tomorrow at 10 AM, Harper Center, Room 3048."

CHAPTER

EIGHT

THE NEXT MORNING as Johnny and Katie entered from the lower level, hundreds of people were standing in the Harper Center hallway outside of room 3048 or climbing the stairs toward it. At the entrance to the room, a table of six students were checking names off an alphabetically organized invitation list. If names were not on the list, they were politely but directly told they were trying to assure everyone who was invited would get a seat, and if they would like to watch the presentation on a remote viewing screen, they could watch in room 3047 down the hall. The students were well prepared, and the line moved efficiently.

Johnny thought to himself that the crowd waiting to get in was remarkably diverse in age, sex, ethnicity and type. He wasn't sure what he expected, but he found it a positive indication that the organizers were paying attention. There was not a lot of chatting but occasional connections between friends from around Omaha and the University broke the calm.

Katie saw a couple of professors she knew, including her PhD advisee, Cara, sitting across the room. Cara stuck her tongue out and made a face when she saw her. "What were they thinking," Katie said quietly to Johnny. They snickered to themselves.

Once in the room, they moved to open seats and could see Andy St. John, Elizabeth Grayson and ten other members of the Society working lap-tops and cell phones on either side of a large screen that was lowered at the back of the stage. None of the Society members were wearing bathrobes or ballcaps. That morning, it was all business, and their attire and bearing matched. Both Katie and Johnny noted the change. Very soon, every seat was filled, the lights were dimmed, and the New Democracy Amendment logo was projected onto the center screen.

Elizabeth Grayson moved confidently into the spotlight and began. "I'd like to welcome all of you to our post-launch organizational meeting. Each of you has gone to our website, signed the petition and volunteered assistance to our cause. I have seen the astonishing matrix of backgrounds and skill sets of the people in this room. From a high-level military staff officer to major players in Fortune 100 corporations and cutting-edge tech start-ups, I've got to tell you, I don't think there has ever been an assembly of such extraordinary talent in one room in the history of Nebraska. Thank you all for coming... For the past three months, the twelve of us on stage have spent nearly every waking hour and a considerable amount of our dream time conceiving this plan to save our country. Save our country. I still get chills. Like you, our inspiration has come from Professor Fletcher. Because of his amazing depth of understanding of the world and a few unimaginable seeds of pure genius that he has given to us to plant, we are committed. However, leading this effort from the very beginning is a man I've grown to love and respect. We are here because of his vision. He saw the potential long before anyone else, and his sheer will and commitment continues to astound us. Ladies and gentlemen, Andrew St. John."

Wearing a tailored grey suit, club tie and well-polished cordovan shoes, Andy affably smiled as he took the light. Elizabeth faded into the shadow.

"She's so dramatic... I'm always surprised when she says my name at the end of all that," Andy said. The crowd smiled and responded well to his self-effacing style. He was brilliantly charismatic without any of the cautionary red flags common to people with such big ambitions. It didn't take long for people to feel as though he was a close personal friend.

"As many of you already know and partly because of the efforts of some of you, social media on the Professor's speech is blowing up. A few minutes ago, our Analytics Team informed us that we had gone well over 1 million visits to the website in the twelve hours since the speech, and the time onsite is off the charts."

There was an audible gasp in the crowd from the people who knew and understood the implication of such numbers in such a short time.

"After today, we won't be meeting much, if at all. Instead, we have a number of communications platforms that will keep us moving in the same direction, but I felt it was important that the nucleus of our leadership meet, at least once, to get a personal sense of our common purpose. This morning I will focus mostly on our Operating Philosophy and our Organizational Model. I'll also go through the various departments and where each of you potentially fits."

Almost everyone in the auditorium pulled open notebooks, laptops or their phones. It was high-tech all the way. There were no political overtones. The sense of things was that this was all purely getting down to business. As Andy spoke, a tech support person flashed detailed bullet points or specific quotes on the central screen to organize and emphasize the presentation. The coordination was well rehearsed.

"Most of the learned people with whom we have discussed the *New Democracy Amendment* and the *Nebraska Strategy,* believe that in concert they could bring about the most important changes to our government since it was conceived. As the professor mentioned, ninety percent of the American public currently view the system as 'broken' and overall disapproval of almost everything the government does is extraordinarily high. That simple reality represents incredible power that can be used to accomplish what needs to be done. The opportunity before us is clear. However, it is important to remember that our success depends not on putting forward a concept that changes our Founder's vision, but rather polishes or reinforces their intent. We want to speak with one clear, simple and human voice that says, 'This is the America we have always been taught to believe in.' If we do this right, we can capture the imagination of the American people and do the impossible," said Andy, emphatically.

"Of course, all of this seems utterly impossible in this era of political polarity, but it is exactly that perception of helplessness that is and always has been the clarion call to the American psyche. We will rally to survive and thrive, as one people, when all of the odds are against us, because we always have. It is one of the most persuasive indicators that we can accomplish what we have set out to do."

"I can tell you, right now, that every major American political ideology is represented in this room. There are Conservatives. There are Libertarians. There are Liberals. And there are wild-eyed Progressives. Yet, all of us have responded to Professor Fletcher's message, and all of us are committed to passing the *New Democracy Amendment*. That's brilliant, and what's really cool is that our primary challenge is not to recraft a message that will sell to a wide range of factions. Our challenge is to present one resoundingly simple, clear and human list of principles that will sell to everyone. We can do that…"

"So, let's get organized. We have borrowed our management philosophy from General Stanley McChrystal's *Team of Teams*. For those of you who are not familiar, it is an approach to management that is so nimble, it minimizes response time from days and hours to near real-time. It is specifically designed to own the unforeseeable by building connectivity and trust between teams at an astonishing level. To accomplish this, everyone must not only understand the mission but instinctively know what needs to be done and feels empowered to do it. This requires complete transparency and constant information sharing. For most of us, this is a cultural sea change, but one that is in complete unison with what we want to accomplish—an American public that is fully aware and fully engaged. Simply put, the *Team of Teams* concept is an organization of trust, shared purpose and shared consciousness. As a matter of fact, we have one of General McChrystal's former staff officers here who has agreed to help us create this important new culture. Colonel Jones, would you mind standing?"

Reluctantly, Johnny stood to a somewhat impressive ovation. When he sat back down, he said, "Shit, these kids are slick."

Katie grinned broadly and responded, "Not bad bro."

Andy continued, "All of the background you need has already been provided to you on the website. Once you understand that, you can develop your own approach to marketing the amendment—*Team of Teams.* However, we feel there are several issues that are vitally important to making this work. With a nod to *Star Trek,* we call them our *Prime Directives.*"

"First, when you are speaking for the *New Democracy Amendment,* do not get sucked into a discussion of specific issues. The economy, immigration, health care, civil rights, gun control or climate change are all enormously important, but the passage of the amendment has nothing directly to do with any of them. Taking sides will only hurt our cause. Stay above the hot buttons and make this point. These issues are all incredibly important to America, but without the *Amendment,* we will never get to anything that makes sense. Passage of the *Amendment* will de-politicized these issues and create an environment where our leaders can once again find trust and common ground to find workable solutions."

People could be seen emphasizing that point on their devices. It made a good deal of sense to everyone.

"Second, the system that has existed for most of our lifetimes has made government illogical, unreasonable and corrupt. The *New Democracy Amendment* will change the system we have into something principled and forward looking. Thus, we gain nothing by hanging onto old paradigms created by the old way of doing things. We gain nothing from personal attacks, old animosities or the idea that we need to blame someone for the situation we are in. Forget the carnage created by the old system and wipe the slate clean. Instead, focus on the *Amendment* as the first step in realizing a positive new future."

"Third, the *New Democracy Amendment* is primarily about eliminating Establishment blockades to high ideals. It is about a shared American consciousness—what we all know is a better way to live. Throughout our history, there have been groups who have not shared equally in the best that America has had to offer. That was wrong, but the way to address these failures is not to divide, assign blame and relive the past. Instead, we need to look forward to a new day of idealism and unbiased inclusion in the whole."

Spontaneous cheers and applause broke out across the audience. Andy waited for it to subside.

"Finally, the *New Democracy Amendment* will no doubt prove to be imperfect as everything is in the march of history. There will be those who will recommend changes or improvements. Various political factions will attempt to push elements of their agenda into its passage in one state or another. If that is allowed, it will ultimately derail our overall goal, and the American people will lose as a result."

"For the last several months, we have vetted this Amendment in very diverse working groups and considered a long list of different approaches, alternatives and suggestions. Ultimately, we decided the best way to approach it was to focus on provisions that would (a) directly address the core problems the Professor discussed in his speech, (b) build everything from a solid foundation of high ideals, and (c) avoid all provisions that would create factional points of conflict."

"Passage will require the overwhelming support of the American public, so as Pete Seeger said, 'We have to keep our eyes on the prize.' Our somewhat exhaustive research has shown that the overwhelming majority of Americans will support the *New Democracy Amendment* in its present form, but even a hint of partisan or ideological change will doom it to failure. This *Amendment* will succeed not because of its perfection, but because it is a simple, clear and human symbol of how our government and society ought to work."

The logic of the *Prime Directives* seemed to take hold of the audience as people could be seen nodding in affirmation. A new screen appeared.

TEAM OF TEAMS

- General Support Team
  Andy St. John

- News & Speakers Bureau Team
  Elizabeth Grayson

- Website & Analytics Team
  Kyle Ito & Earle Lionberger

- Social Media—Communications Team
  Ella Lamb & Garrett Seltzer

- Video, YouTube & Audio Team
  Mya Kelly & Colon Olsen

- Nebraska Ratification Team
  Connor Babbitt

- National Ratification Team
  Nora Kunkle

- Legal Team
  Josh Byers

- Merchandizing Team
  Kylie Perry

"Let me turn now to how we've structured our *Team of Teams* and how each of you potentially fits in," said Andy. "Let me first say that the organizing committee—our Society of Robes—is fully aware that our skill sets are nowhere near as accomplished as almost every one of you in this room. However, what we have done that you have not is spent the last few months putting in an amazing amount of head time on this project. What I am trying to say is that our intent from here on is to facilitate the best way we know how and to encourage each of you to rise to a level of leadership and involvement that makes sense for you. Show us a better way, and we look forward to following. View us as facilitators, and view everyone here as one passionate team moving toward a common goal."

"So, our *Website & Analytics Team* is led by Kyle Ito and Earle Lionberger. A handful of grad students have been helping them, but after last night, we've added more than a dozen of you with specific expertise who we think might be very helpful. Ella Lamb and Garrett Seltzer are leading the *Social Media–Communications Team*: Facebook, Twitter, Instagram, etc. This group has proven to be highly skilled, but again, we've added a few of you who we think could expand this team's talent pool exponentially. Mya Kelly and Colon Olsen are currently leading the *Video, YouTube & Audio Team*. All three of these teams have overlapped and worked together through rapidly changing circumstances. Those of you who have been added to these teams, if you think you might be more useful in another area, or see something we have not thought of, please let us know. *Team of Teams*—change, adapt, improve, move toward the goal. Get 'r done."

"Josh Byers, soon to begin his first year at Stanford Law, with the help of Professor Sullivan at Creighton Law School has already started to organize infrastructure for our *Legal Team*. We anticipate some interesting challenges on this score, and several of you attorneys and a couple of professors have communicated an interest in participating here. Elizabeth Grayson, who you've all met, is heading our *News & Speakers Bureau Team*. She's been preparing for this for some time, and we suspect will be moving into action very soon. Several of you have voiced an interest in helping here, so she will bring you up to speed."

"For the past several weeks Connor Babbitt has been recruiting and organizing leadership from both college Republican and Democrat organizations in Nebraska. Further, he has approached several former Nebraska State Senators from both parties to create the beginnings of a campaign to ratify the amendment in Nebraska. A rather large number of you last night expressed an interest in helping on that front. We're hoping that the attention, which is mounting, will begin moving this ball forward very quickly. In fact, it's been suggested we may be able to inspire a special session so that Nebraska is guaranteed the honor of being the first state to ratify the *Amendment*."

"For the past several weeks, Nora Kunkle, who is leading the National Ratification Team, has been preparing email and phone contact lists for every Governor and every State Legislator in the United States, as well as a select list of business and political leaders nationwide. Later today, emails with all relevant attachments will drop to them. We've added a bunch of you to assist there. We even have a couple of folks with national presidential campaign experience."

"Possibly, the most rewarding of all of our teams will be the *Merchandizing Team*," Andy said, smiling. "Kylie Perry has graciously agreed to lead this team and several of you seemed to fit the team's needs. "Last and least of all, I'll be leading the *General Support Team*. Essentially, it's our job to solve problems and get you what you need to succeed. I've selected a few of you to join me, but again, if you think you would be more useful somewhere else, we'll make it happen."

"Moving forward, communications will come from a combination of sources. If everything works as intended, all of you should immediately be brought into a continuous loop of information. However, only you will be able to decide how intrusive you want this communication to be. In a moment, each of you will receive a text informing you what team you have been assigned to and the location of a break-out meeting room. There you will be brought up to speed. You will have help putting these pieces together, and you will be given some time to do some brainstorming. Remember, our overall goals are: 1. Educating the public. 2. Maximizing positive media coverage. 3. Gaining ratification of the *Amendment* in Nebraska. 4. Gaining ratification of the *Amendment* in thirty-seven or more other states and making the *28th Amendment* to the

Constitution of the United States of America a reality. I look forward to joining all of you for our first ratification party. Bonne chance mes amis."

As he finished his words, Andy flicked his finger in the air as if he were flipping on a light switch. As he did, text notification signals began to bleep all over the room. He smiled broadly as everyone immediately began looking at their phones.

Johnny looked down. His text said, "Welcome to the General Support Team. Stay put. We're meeting in room 3048." While he was reading, Katie's phone bleeped with a text saying exactly the same thing. They looked at each other's texts and said almost at the same time, "Shit, these kids are slick."

Twelve people stayed behind in room 3048. Andy welcomed each one graciously, interjecting something personal to each of them. When he came to Johnny, he said, "You're Colonel Jones?"

"My age gave me away?" responded Johnny, noticing that he was at least a decade older than most everyone in the room.

"Actually, I Googled you," responded Andy chuckling. Recognizing the Colonel's familiarity with Katie, he continued, "Doctor Duffy, do you two know each other?"

"Yes," said Katie. "I live next door to an old friend of his. We met at their Fourth of July party."

Grinning broadly, Andy remarked, "Excellent, I cannot tell you how many truly serendipitous things have happened similar to that since this whole thing began. Sometimes, I feel like I'm just along for the ride."

Andy seemed very familiar with the remaining men and women in the room—a group that seemed exceptionally young, polished and professional. When he was through, he asked everyone to take a seat at a large table that had been organized on the stage.

After everyone had taken a seat, he began. "The *General Support Committee* is intended, as the name implies, to provide general support to the overall effort. We will try to be problem solvers as well as provide as much strategic planning as possible. This is somewhat of a dubious charge, as I have the expectation we will probably be running as fast as we can just to keep up. If we have time to think, my guess is this effort probably isn't going where we want it to… Besides Colonel Jones and Professor Duffy, who were added after last night's speech, the rest of you have been in the loop for several weeks. You were chosen because of your relative youth; your early success in your chosen industry; and your connection to the top corporations in Nebraska—Berkshire Hathaway, Tenaska, Union Pacific, Gallup, Kiewit, TD Ameritrade, First Data, etc."

"I grew up in the business world. My dad was an investment banker here in Omaha, and I got to know a lot of his business friends and their families. Over the years I recognized that the overwhelming majority of them were extraordinarily principled people who cared deeply about the world around them. They were not in any way the clichés of greed and corruption that are so often portrayed by the media. It is my belief that though many of them participate in the Establishment in some way, they view this participation as a necessary evil—a requirement of doing business in an era dominated by corruption and dirty politics."

"My Dad tells a story of a business venture in which he participated in Ukraine after the fall of the Soviet Union. While the deal was being explained, he was struck by how few of the participants paid attention to the details. Later, as all but the principals left the room, he was very affably but pointedly asked to explain how it would all really work. In other words, how and to whom would the payoffs be distributed. You see, in their world, the agreement, the contract didn't really matter. What mattered was who would take care of who under the table. That moment was an epiphany for my father. He realized then that what had truly made America great was a business environment that was based on truth, principle and ethical conduct. In his mind, it was rare in the world. Bad actors, always a few, but the American business community was and is the infrastructure that has always made this nation special."

"It is my firm belief, using the talents and connections represented on this stage, we can convince this nation's business leaders that not only is the *New Democracy Amendment* good for the people, it will be extremely good for business. Reconfiguring a principle made by Robert

Hall and Alvin Rabushka in their *Flat Tax* theory, if you repurpose all the money business is forced to use in dealing with bogus government taxes, intrusions and political nonsense, and reapply it to solid business investment, it would be like a rocket ship for the American economy."

"This is how I think things will track from here. Already the Professor's speeches and the *Amendment* are trending. Right after lunch, we will begin a strategic surge of information across every major platform. Weekend news desk people will clearly identify that something is happening and will start putting together the facts. Some of them will begin organizing stories and maybe start calling their bosses at home. At some point, one of the news organizations will dig deep enough to realize that this proposal could change everything and that will be the flashpoint."

"What I would like each of you to do is to go into your business contact lists and let them know ahead of time that something big is coming—something that could change their world. Sell them. Convince them they need to get out in front of it and support it. Give them ownership. Our greatest challenge is that the average person on the street will see themselves as too insignificant to help. If we can get Mr. Buffett and the rest of your bosses to start reaching out in support, I think it could be the boost of confidence this whole thing needs to succeed. That's what I want you to do. Build your own campaigns and bring them home."

Each of the other people in the room went around expressing some variation of the concept that the *Amendment* was the most important political event in their lifetime and could possibly be a seminal moment in the nation's history—when the goals of our Founding Fathers were truly realized. The most dramatic moment in the room that day was when everyone individually realized at roughly the same time that they were surrounded by people every bit as brilliant as they were, and they collectively shared as uncommon affirmation of extraordinary expectation.

CHAPTER
NINE

AS PREDICTED, the national media began to pick up the story. By Saturday afternoon, online media sources were blowing up. Later in the afternoon, interns and junior producers at the cable networks were reading the details of the *Amendment* and watching the Professor's speeches. It was having an impact, but the senior producers and on-air personalities were largely still unaware of the details. By Saturday evening, the story was trending strongly with younger journalists nationwide and favorable opinion was growing. By Sunday morning, the major network newsrooms were discussing it and assigning reporters. By Sunday afternoon, FOX, CNN and MSNBC were all making mention of the *Amendment* on air and showing excerpts from the Professor's speeches. By Sunday evening, every major news organization in America was looking into the details and contacting Elizabeth and the News Team for quotes, which had already been prepared. By Monday, early morning shows were making mention of the *Nebraska Strategy* for passing a constitutional amendment, and by 9 AM, Elizabeth and three members of her team were walking out of the *Jewel Hotel* opposite Rockefeller Center ready for a day of interviews.

In spite of the genuine excitement being generated by younger producers and reporters at the time, Elizabeth's first appearances were rocky. Like the Native Americans who first viewed Columbus' ships on the horizon, the more experienced and cynical news commentators were having a difficult time wrapping their heads around what they were seeing. How could such idealism be real? In her first few shows, lead commentators were fully prepared with all their smarmy condescension to expose the entire movement as a fraud.

"You say the system is broken, but don't we have a system in place to fix that? It's called an election."

"We just had an election and all it did was move us closer to civil war. Look, everyone can see the system is broken. In every election cycle, candidates use some variation of 'we need change' in their slogan and nothing ever changes. It only gets worse. The truth is elections and the money that fuels them are the problem. Whether it's rich individuals or interest groups, money controls every aspect of our electoral process, and it is far more powerful than the people. The only way to make our votes count again is to get as much money out of the process as possible."

"Constitutional Amendments have been proposed many times before, what's so different about your effort?"

It's not tainted from the start. Our method of proposing an amendment, the *Nebraska Strategy*, is an end-run around the corruption of the system. Our amendment has not been proposed to preserve greed, but to allow the clear-eyed will of the people to be realized.

"Your Professor was certainly hard on journalists. What did he say, 'The truth is it's all fake news'? Sounds like a Donald Trump line to me."

"You ask Liberals and Progressives if the journalists at FOX News are honest, and they will tell you, *Hell No*, and go off from there. Conversely, if you ask Conservatives if CNN, MSNBC and the mainstream media are honest, they will blow-up in your face. The truth is that neither side is getting the whole truth, and that allows viewers to conclude the other side is lying. It's all just a game, and the American people are sick of it."

"Why in the world do you think Republicans would support this Amendment? Aren't they the party of big business?"

"If you look at the numbers and who the donors are, any impartial observer will tell you that both political parties are heavily influenced by big business, but you shouldn't limit your observations to just business. The balance sheet of both parties is overloaded with unsavory influencers with genuinely corrupt motives. We believe the Establishment is any individual or entity who wants to manipulate government for its own benefit, and both political parties are equally guilty of complicity."

"Now, you seem to be singing the song of Congresswoman Ocasio-Cortez?"

"In some ways I am, and that is the primary reason she is so popular in spite of pushing a largely socialist agenda. But the bigger issue is, a growing number of Americans on both the right and the left see how big money is corrupting the system. They share a lot of similar ideas, and the media has largely missed it. We're putting forward a constitutional amendment that is founded solidly on that common ground."

"Section 1 of your new Amendment is all warm and fuzzy, but come-on, you can't make Americans better people just by passing an amendment."

"Couldn't agree more, and this isn't about a few words on paper. This is about honest to gosh virtue. You know the real thing? Most of us, even poor little African American girls like me, grew up hearing and maybe even believing in truth, sacrifice, courage and honor. But today, we don't hear much about virtue, and many of us have forgotten just how important it is to a functioning democracy. If we want to rid our nation of corruption and oligarchy, we need to start believing in principle again. No, Section 1 isn't a magic wand, but it is a great big symbol to rally around and say, *Hey, let's get our act together.*"

"You know, a lot of what you say has merit, but we've been trying to take the money out of politics for a long, long time. Why do you think you can succeed when no one else has?"

"The Founding Fathers had to wheel and deal to get the Constitution ratified, and frankly, they had too much faith in the elite. Almost from the beginning, the rich and powerful used their influence to get a bigger share of the pie. Many statutory efforts have been undertaken over the years to regain control, but without a Constitutional Amendment, real change is impossible. This time we're starting from a legal foundation originated in the *Declaration of Independence,* and we're going to pass an amendment by sheer will of the people. It's never been done before, but we will go around Congress and the Establishment, and give ourselves a new nation based on a renewed sense of idealism."

"But doesn't his idea fly directly in the face of Article V? Isn't going around Article V kind of an inauspicious way to pass an amendment of such magnitude?"

"Absolutely not. It's just the opposite. Our effort is completely consistent with the mind and spirit of our Founding Fathers. Legal scholars have long suggested that Article V is merely a process whereby the government can amend the Constitution, and the *Declaration of Independence* makes it absolutely clear that the will of the people supersedes all authority. *We the People* are the government, and what we are doing is exactly what the Founding Fathers did in the original ratification process. They went around the *Articles of Confederation* to pass the *Constitution*, because the people wanted and needed a better system of government. Everything we are doing fits perfectly with the intent and tradition of our founding."

"Let's get into some of the practical problems if your amendment passes. Fact, political campaigns cost billions of dollars to elect people to office. If you eliminate all of the organizational money from campaigns, who is going to pay for them, or do you intend to have them funded by the government?"

"Absolutely not. Preliminary research suggests that the funding of political campaigns will drop by at least ninety percent if our

Amendment passes. Think about that. No more money for opposition research, endless radio and television commercials, dirty tricks, forest leveling direct mail campaigns or outrageous cyber intrusions. People will have to run on reputation, experience and issues. Candidates will need to work their way up by distinguishing themselves in business or local government, and once again local journalists will help guide voters to sensible conclusions instead of being led around by the nose. In fact, the whole thing might look a lot like our Founding Fathers intended."

"In Section 2, hidden in the middle, there is a rule that prohibits candidates contributing to their own campaigns beyond a common limit. How can you tell someone what they can and can't do with their own money?"

"Does a rich man or woman deserve a better shot at elected office just because of his or her wealth? The people overwhelmingly don't think so. The wealthy will still have many significant advantages, but they will have to raise money like everyone else to be competitive.

"Okay, but do you think the wealthy will support your effort to ratify this Amendment?"

"Overwhelmingly so. Most wealthy people in this country are good Americans. They will support the Amendment because it's the right thing to do. And they will really appreciate not having a constant barrage of people hitting them up for large contributions. They may end-up being this effort's biggest cheerleaders."

"In the end, who do you think this Amendment will really favor?"

"The American People. Look, this Amendment is about nothing more than breaking down the barriers to good, honest and fair government. It's about taking down a system that is undermining our democracy. The only side it takes is the people's."

"In his first speech, the Professor used the term "realcapital." I've heard of realpolitik before, but not realcapital?"

"It's the Professor's invention. As you know, *realpolitik* is a term or movement that essentially takes a real-world approach to government. What *realcapital* suggests is that there are always economic winners and losers in any form of government. A socialist or communist state suggests they are all about equality, but in truth economic reward is based on loyalty to the party. In capitalism, reward is based on productivity. The point is economic reward is always there. The difference lies in how it is rewarded—*realcapital*."

"Can you explain what you mean by the *New Democracy Amendment* fostering an 'evolution' in democracy?"

"Great question, and one that frequently gets glossed over. At the dawn of democracy, Cleisthenes presented every Athenian with a black rock and a white rock to give each citizen an equal say in decisions. Over time, individual rights were introduced as a balance to the power of the majority. That was an evolutionary step in democracy. Over more time, the right to vote was dramatically expanded. That was another evolutionary step. By Constitutionally prohibiting the corrupting influences of money in our electoral process, we will be saying for the first time that using money to subvert the democratic process is unacceptable, and it will be another evolutionary step forward for democracy."

"Realistically, do you think the *New Democracy Amendment* will have any real impact on people who want to use their money to cheat the system?"

"We'll always have criminals and cheats. What this Amendment will do is make it absolutely clear who they are."

"One last question, if you are successful in using your *Nebraska Strategy to* pass this Amendment, what's to stop any wild-eyed radical from passing any number of nutty amendments?"

"Another great question! Really great question. This strategy changes nothing in the difficulty of ratifying amendments to the Constitution.

Three-fourths of the states, 38 states, were required for ratification last year, and 38 states will be required for ratification going forward. All the *Nebraska Strategy* does is cut out Establishment control of the process and give it back to the people."

* * *

After Elizabeth's first two appearances on cable news, the movement to ratify the *New Amendment* was never looked at the same way again. A new day was emerging in America, and once again the United States turned the world upside down.

Is this the end or the beginning?
It's your call.

ADDENDUM 1: THE NEW DEMOCRACY AMENDMENT

Amendment XXVIII
to the Constitution of the United States of America

1: It shall be the duty of the people, the media, and the government of the United States to act in the spirit of the twelve common virtues of citizenship. These virtues are: *Truth* as the path to understanding; *Faith* in the goodness of humankind; *Sacrifice* for the greater good; *Frugality* in the avoidance of waste; *Balance* to avoid the corruption of extremes; *Discipline* to search for excellence; *Diligence* in overcoming adversity; *Civility* in the preservation of unity; *Justice* in demonstrating equality under the law; *Humility* in the control of pride; *Courage* to stand alone for right; and the *Honor* to live on principle, even in solitude."

2: No financial or organizational support, whatsoever, shall move from any organization, interest group, union, or business interest of any kind to support or oppose any candidate for local, state, or federal office. All money contributed to local, state, or federal campaigns for office shall be contributed solely by individual donors with a permanent residence within the specific geographic area to be represented and shall be deposited directly to a respective candidate's campaign committee. No contribution, including those made by the candidate, shall exceed $2,000 in a primary election and $2,000 in a general election. All campaign contributions must be drawn from personal assets and be publicly recorded with the appropriate oversight body within twenty-four hours of the contribution. The record shall include the date and time, donor's name and address, and the amount contributed.

3: All persons employed by the government of the United States, including those serving in elected, appointed, or military positions, shall receive no gifts, compensation, employment, promise of employment, or any other incentive from companies, individuals, or countries doing business with the government of the United States. This prohibition shall continue until a term of two years after the employee, or elected, appointed, or military personnel, leaves government service.

4: All organizations, interest groups, unions, business interests, or individuals desirous of influencing the laws and policies of the United States shall be strictly limited to providing written information to the various government entities.

Article V of the Constitution of the United States:

The Congress, whenever two thirds of both houses shall deem it necessary, shall propose amendments to this Constitution, or, on the application of the legislatures of two thirds of the several states, shall call a convention for proposing amendments, which, in either case, shall be valid to all intents and purposes, as part of this Constitution, when ratified by the legislatures of three fourths of the several states, or by conventions in three fourths thereof, as the one or the other mode of ratification may be proposed by the Congress; provided that no amendment which may be made prior to the year one thousand eight hundred and eight shall in any manner affect the first and fourth clauses in the ninth section of the first article; and that no state, without its consent, shall be deprived of its equal suffrage in the Senate.

ADDENDUM 2:
NEBRASKA STRATEGY

Suppose one state legislature passes an Amendment intended for inclusion in the Constitution of the United States, and then thirty-seven more state legislatures pass the same amendment by the sheer weight of its popularity and wisdom. Clearly, the test of the *Will of the People* would have been satisfied through the ultimate requirement for ratification. However, would the fact that it did not first go through the formal requirement for proposal established in Article V be enough to render the ratification null? We don't think so. The *Will of the People* is and always has been the ultimate authority in the United States of America.

The proposal process explained in Article V, through a Congressional or Convention of States mechanism, has long been criticized by constitutional scholars as unrealistically encumbered. Many have suggested there are other methods of introducing constitutional amendments which are within the power of the people, and that Article V is merely the exclusive way for the government to go about it. Scholars support their conclusion by pointing out that the Founding Fathers themselves used this justification to ratify the Constitution in the first place. They bypassed the procedures established by the *Articles of Confederation* and succeeded in ratification through the popular support of the people.

The power of the people and the power of states have been clearly established from the earliest references in Constitutional law. Thomas Jefferson said specifically in the *Declaration of Independence,* "That whenever any Form of Government becomes destructive of these ends, it is the Right of the People to alter or abolish it, and to institute new

Government, laying its foundation on such principles and organizing its powers in such form, as to them shall seem the most likely to effect their Safety and Happiness."

Clearly, the Founding Fathers intended the people to have the ultimate power to create the laws under which they live. Ratifying amendments to the Constitution in accordance with the final standard set by the Constitution, a three-fourths majority of State Legislatures, would seem to supersede any procedural issue of lesser importance.

Statistically speaking, the democratic mechanism that most clearly reflects the *Will of the People* should satisfy any lesser issues in question. Currently, 535 men and women serve in the Congress of the United States, and 7,383 men and women serve the same people in state legislatures across the United States. Surely, the ultimate decision of a three-fourths majority of 7,383 state legislators, who are in every practical way closer to the people, should supersede a two-thirds majority of 535 members of Congress that are strictly limited to voting on a procedural motion. The three-fourth majority of state legislatures that are required for ratification of amendments to the Constitution is sufficient to meet any mandate the Founding Fathers intended.

Currently, the National Archives and Records Administration is responsible for administering the ratification of amendments. According to the Archives, "Neither Article V of the Constitution nor section 106b describes the ratification process in detail. The Archivist and Director of the Federal Register simply follow the procedures and customs set by earlier Secretary of States who held these duties prior to 1950." Again, according to the Archives, "In the past, some State Legislatures have not waited to receive official notice before taking action on a proposed amendment." They have either supported or rejected an amendment before it was ever officially proposed, and their actions have been upheld. There is precedent in ratifying amendments in State Legislatures prior to their official proposal.

Article V gives the ultimate power for adoption or rejection of amendments to the States, rather than to the Congress, to which is given only procedural authority, and even that authority can be substituted by again, State authority. Theoretically, if need be, the States could first ratify amendments, and then organize a Convention of States to propose the amendments retroactively. Again, the States have the ultimate say.

Finally, to address the argument that bypassing the procedures specified in Article V could open "a can of worms" in the amendment process: No matter what amendments may be proposed, a three-fourths majority of state legislatures still must ratify these amendments to make them law. It is one thing to propose an outlandish change to our Constitution. It is quite another to gain ratification. Case in point: Six amendments to the Constitution have been duly proposed by Congress but have not made it through the ratification process. A three-fourths majority of state legislatures has proven to be a more than adequate barometer of the *Will of the People* over the past 233 years.

www.BigWalnutCreek.com

Made in the USA
Monee, IL
07 June 2023

35420614R00069